All for You

USA TODAY BESTSELLING AUTHOR

Heather B. Moore

All for You

A PINE VALLEY NOVEL

Copyright © 2019 by Heather B. Moore
Print edition
All rights reserved

No part of this book may be reproduced in any form whatsoever without prior written permission of the publisher, except in the case of brief passages embodied in critical reviews and articles. This is a work of fiction. The characters, names, incidents, places, and dialogue are products of the author's imagination and are not to be construed as real.

Interior design by Cora Johnson
Edited by Kelsey Down and Lisa Shepherd
Cover design by Rachael Anderson
Cover image credit: Deposit Photos #73479323, Belchonock
Published by Mirror Press, LLC
ISBN-13: 978-1-947152-61-8

PINE VALLEY SERIES

Worth the Risk
Where I Belong
Say You Love Me
Waiting for You
Finding Us
Until We Kissed
Let's Begin Again
All for You

All for You

Life has always been about the game for pro hockey player Tyler Nelson, but when he meets attorney Lindsey Gerber, Tyler discovers his feelings for Lindsey are anything but a game.

Crash and burn pretty much describes Lindsey Gerber's last six months at her law firm, where she hoped to make partner. Now, every goal she's made is suddenly out the window. She moves to Pine Valley, looking for a new start. On day one, she meets pro hockey player Tyler Nelson, who's recovering from an injury and in a physical therapy program that includes nature things like hiking the ski resort, which he makes no secret of hating. He also makes no secret of his interest in Lindsey. Their lives are two worlds apart, though, and it will take one of them changing everything to make a relationship work.

One

"I don't know, Dawson," Lindsey Gerber said into the phone as she gazed at the San Francisco morning fog three stories below her corner office. "Pine Valley is like another world. And rumor is that you're the big man in town."

Dawson Harris chuckled in that low, warm tone of his.

Lindsey sighed at the sound of his laugh. One, because it was good to talk to a friend. Two, because it reminded her that she hadn't laughed or enjoyed much of anything for a very long time. Six months and three days, to be exact, since starting at Perkins & Gunner.

She and Dawson had been in law school together. He'd had her back when one of their professors hit on her during their first year. She'd helped him avoid a crazy stalker ex-girlfriend during their second year. Despite Dawson being unarguably the best-looking man in law school, they'd never dated. He was like the brother she'd never had.

And Dawson said that Lindsey was one of the few people

he could be himself around, although "being himself" was still pretty much twenty steps ahead of everyone else. If there was any phrase to describe Dawson Harris, it was "the golden touch." And now he was trying to convince her to quit her firm, move to the mountain-resort town of Pine Valley, lease his extra office space, and set up her own law practice. In theory, she could pick up and move. She didn't have any family in the area. Her elderly father lived in San Diego.

"Are estate-planning lawyers in demand in Pine Valley?" Lindsey asked.

"You've helped out more than one of my clients, long distance," Dawson said. "You know you can do a lot with email and FedEx."

Lindsey rubbed at the back of her sore neck. Yep. It was seven thirty in the morning, and she was already tired and achy. Might have something to do with the fact that she'd been working on a case until one in the morning, then she woke up at five and couldn't get back to sleep. She'd gotten on the BART carrying her second cup of coffee and a laptop full of endless work and knowing she'd be in board meetings all afternoon with the partners of the company. One of whom had been texting her at odd hours, getting more and more personal. She hadn't told Dawson about Paul because she knew he'd come unglued.

When Dawson had called a few minutes ago, Lindsey almost hadn't answered the phone. She didn't want her current mood to clue Dawson in on how miserable she was. She hated to complain, and she was a firm believer in having control over one's happiness. But Dawson's call had come in a moment of great weakness, because his offer was sounding very tempting. She had to stay strong, though. Partner at a major law firm had been her goal since she started her undergraduate degree.

"I'm on track to make partner here," she continued. "Mr. Gunner pretty much told me it's in the bag—a few more months at the most." But even as she tried to put a cheerful note in her voice, her stomach felt tight.

Dawson didn't hesitate before answering. "You'll make partner, Lindsey. You're amazing."

She wanted to smile at the confidence in his voice, let it buoy her up. But she only felt more miserable. "Thanks," she said, her throat sounding thick. She had to get off with him in case the burning in her eyes turned into actual tears. "I gotta go. Good luck selling that lease."

When she hung up with Dawson, she didn't move for a few moments as she stared across the gray murkiness that covered the bay. She'd been to Pine Valley a couple of times to attend the attorney retreats Dawson had put together. The retreats were collaboration events where lawyers from different specialties would interact, listen to presentations, and discuss new laws, and in the end, most of them would end up referring clients to each other.

Dawson was always in the know, always networking, always looking out for others, including Lindsey.

A text buzzed, and Lindsey looked down at her phone.

Hey, Lind, want anything from Einstein's?

Paul Locker. His attentions were getting more and more intrusive.

She didn't want to see him today, but there was no way she could get out of the board meeting, not if she wanted to make partner. And if she didn't find a way to shake off Paul, he'd be showing up in her office in about twenty minutes.

No, thanks. I've eaten, and I'm trying to get through a review before lunch. She hit SEND, then groaned when he wrote right back.

That's my girl. Always working. I'm impressed.

She wasn't a girl, and her name wasn't Lind. If anyone else talked to her this way, she probably wouldn't be so annoyed, but everything that Paul did bothered her. He was just so fake, smooth, like a villain in a cartoon. It would be comical, if it weren't happening to her.

Lindsey moved away from the window and sat down at her desk. Picking up a thick file, she began to leaf through her notes. Mrs. Grady had only been married to her software-mogul husband for three months, but his will clearly indicated that she was to receive the estate. Other holdings went to his three adult children. Mr. Grady had died in a small plane crash, and now the children from his first marriage were trying to run Mrs. Grady off the estate.

The law was the law, and the will had been drawn. Even if the ink hadn't been dry, the legality still held up. Lindsey would make sure everyone understood that Mrs. Grady was the new owner of the estate and that the harassment needed to stop. Lindsey spent the next few hours working on the case and fielding several phone calls.

Someone tapped on her door, then opened it. The prickles running along her neck told her who it was before she saw him.

"I brought you lunch," Paul said in that smooth tone of his.

Lindsey looked up, blinking against the headache that had concentrated itself behind her left temple. A quick glance at the ornate clock on the wall told her that it was indeed lunch time.

Paul wore one of his signature bow ties today, along with a suit in a herringbone pattern. Lindsey supposed the look might be attractive to some women, but not her. Yes, his blonde hair and bright-blue eyes were appealing. But the white flash of his teeth and his regular trips to the tanning salon brought out the photoshopped, fake look.

"Before you say you're too busy to eat, I brought your favorite."

Lindsey could smell the Japanese food a mile away, and she almost smiled. Because now that she smelled the food, she realized she was starving. But . . . Paul . . .

He grinned and pulled a chair close to her desk, so they were sitting opposite of each other. Then with a practiced flourish, he pulled out three cartons of food from a large delivery sack, then a couple of chilled water bottles that he'd probably snagged from the break room, and finally napkins and chopsticks.

"Thanks, Paul," she said, grabbing her purse from the shelf behind her. "What do I owe you?"

He chuckled. It wasn't the warm chuckle of Dawson. More of a suggestive chuckle. Was that a thing?

"I like the way you think, Lind." Paul unwrapped his chopsticks. "Let's just say that you never have to pay me for anything."

Lindsey felt the prickle again. She reached for the wallet in her purse and pulled out a twenty-dollar bill, grateful she had cash. "Here," she said, handing it over. "Thanks again."

Paul reached out his hand, but instead of taking the money, he wrapped his fingers over hers. "Lind, come on. Lunch is on me. And anything else you want to be on me."

She blinked, because she wasn't quite sure he was saying . . .

Paul's fingers tightened over hers, and his gaze moved from her face to her neck, then lower. She was wearing a V-neck blouse, fitted but perfectly modest. But by the way Paul was scanning her, she didn't feel so covered up.

"I love that necklace on you," he said.

Her other hand went to her throat. She was wearing one of her mom's necklaces. And Paul was still holding her hand. She pulled away, but his grip only tightened.

"Wait, Lind," he said. "I need to tell you something."

She tugged harder. He didn't need to hold her hand to tell her something. He let go, but there was triumph in his eyes, as if he knew how much he'd affected her. He just didn't know it was in the *wrong* way.

Her skin felt flushed, and her heart rate was zooming. She didn't know whether to chew him out or leave the office. She swallowed, but before she could speak, he said, "I think we'd be good together," he said. "You're ambitious, and I'm a partner."

"Paul, I hope you're not going to say what I think you are." She hated that her voice was trembling.

He arched one of his tweezed brows. Yep. He tweezed. Had told her about it once. "I want to say a lot of things," he said in a smooth voice, "but we don't spend nearly enough time together for me to get them all out. And that's what I'm proposing we change."

Lindsey gripped the edges of her desk. The scent of the Japanese food no longer made her hungry; it made her nauseated.

"Have you ever heard of the proverbial good ole boys' club?" he asked.

"Of course."

His smile was back. Magazine ready. "You know how the legal world is. Men on top, women on bottom. But we can change that, for *you*, at least."

"With hard work and successful cases?" Lindsey said. The trembling was replaced by rising anger. She couldn't believe she'd allowed this man to even walk into her office.

"Have you ever heard the phrase, 'You rub my back, I'll rub yours'?" Paul winked.

She stood. "You need to leave now."

Paul didn't even seem surprised at her request, which

only irked her more. "Chill, Lind. We're only having lunch and discussing office politics."

She took a shaky breath, her stomach feeling like it was about to flip over. Crossing to the door, she opened it a few inches. "You have thirty seconds, Paul."

His smile faded. He carefully, slowly, set down his chopsticks, then pushed up from his chair.

Lindsey kept her gaze on the opposite wall, not even wanting to look into his eyes. But he didn't leave, not yet. He paused by her and leaned in. Inhaled slowly. "You're playing with fire, sweetheart." He ran his thumb along her jaw, and she jerked away.

He merely chuckled. "You really don't want to piss me off. So drink some of that cold water, and I'll see you in the board room. Hopefully by the end of our meetings, you'll be ready to apologize, *if* you want that partnership. Gunner and I go way back, and I'll win out every time."

She opened the door wider, and when he finally stepped through, she shut the door. Then leaned against it, closing her eyes. She wouldn't cry. Not now. But despite her resolve, her throat felt like she'd swallowed gravel, and her hands were trembling again. She needed to report Paul. But where would that leave her? Without a job. She knew, everyone knew, there was a good ole boys' club at most of these law firms.

She'd file a complaint, Paul would receive a warning, her cases would start to dwindle, the money she brought into the firm would be cut in half, and by the time the end-of-year review came around, no one would vote for her. And what if, by some miracle, she was made partner? She'd have to spend every day she was in the office trying to avoid Paul. Which would be impossible. Even if he ignored her, she would *feel* his disdain. She'd feel cheap, worthless.

These realizations were nothing new—had been plaguing

her for weeks ever since Paul had decided that he had permission to text her outside of work hours.

Lindsey wiped at her cheeks, then crossed to her desk. Using the Japanese takeout sack, she put in her personal effects from about the office. Then she packed up her laptop into her computer bag. Finally, she grabbed her purse. She'd email in her resignation.

For now, she walked out of the office, past a handful of closed office doors, past the glass-walled conference room. Naomi, the firm's receptionist, was setting out water bottles on the long oval table. Lindsey continued down the hall until she reached the elevator. She pushed the lobby button, and as the elevator descended, she texted Dawson Harris.

Is that lease still available?

Two

"This is bullsh—"

"*Positivity*, Nelson," Maddy said, her singsong voice like a mother speaking to a five-year-old kid. "Our *words* become our thoughts, and our *thoughts* become our actions. When the frustration builds inside of you, remember to push out the negativity." She swept her hands from her chest outward. "*Push it out...*"

Tyler Nelson clenched his jaw. Not only did his body ache from trying to keep up with his physical therapist turned wellness coach, Maddy Hardy—emphasis on *Hard*—as she goat climbed this freaking mountain, but the playoffs were in three weeks. That meant he had to be back to his pre-injury form and on the ice in two weeks. If he couldn't prove to Coach that he was ready to return to his goaltender spot on the Vegas Falcons, the professional hockey team, Ben would stay in.

The Falcons were picked to win the Stanley Cup this year.

But first, they had to cut a wide berth through the playoffs. And Nelson would be dam—er, *darned* if that happened without him. Now, looking up the slope he was currently climbing as part of his wilderness physical therapy, Nelson grimaced at the bits of snow that still clung to the rocks and dead grass. The cold spring of Pine Valley hadn't done anything to loosen up his joints and muscles. He missed Vegas's warmer weather.

He pulled out his water bottle from his backpack and took a swig.

"You should have finished that water bottle by now," Maddy said. "What did I tell you about drinking fluids?"

Nelson continued to chug, finishing the thing off. "Happy?" He glanced over at Maddy.

She smirked. The woman was all of five foot one and at least forty years old, although it was hard to know since she was one of those all-natural types. No makeup, no painted nails, no jewelry, no hair dye. Bits of gray streaked her dark hair. All Nelson really knew about her was that Coach thought she walked on water with her pseudo-natural-holistic-whatever physical therapy strategies.

This was why he was currently hundreds of miles away from home, hiking in cold slush. Surrounded by elements of nature such as giant pine trees, dead pine needles, and rotting aspen leaves.

Spring was definitely coming, but Nelson wouldn't be around here long enough to see anything worth his trouble.

"Almost there," Maddy said. "Maybe fifty more yards. Then we're zigzagging down so that you don't put too much stress on your knees."

It was his left knee that he'd tweaked in a game last week as he collided with a three-hundred-pound forward from the Seattle Blacks hockey team. Nelson had gone down hard but had still managed to make the save. The Falcons had won two to one.

The game was over in three more minutes, and Nelson had done everything he could to stay in the game, including nearly biting through his mouth guard. He didn't want to tell Coach about the strain in his knee, but the guy was observant and saw him limping after he got off the ice.

Thankfully, an MRI showed no tearing, only swelling. They'd called it a grade-one medial collateral ligament sprain. Thus the mandatory physical therapy with nature-loving Maddy.

"Let's do it," Nelson said, knowing that going up meant that later he could come down. And eat something more than the protein shake and weird chia-seed granola Maddy had given him that morning.

Nelson pushed through the throbbing of his knee as he climbed. Despite his complaining about the physical therapy, he could feel the recovery starting. The swelling had gone down, and things felt more stable all the way around. He obeyed Maddy and finished off his second water bottle. So by the time they reached the top, then—sure enough—zigzagged to the bottom of the ski slope, Nelson was good and hungry.

They climbed into Maddy's Subaru Outback—a vehicle that seemed to fit her perfectly. Not so much Nelson. The passenger seat was quite a bit smaller than his truck back in Vegas. A guy like him, over two hundred pounds and six foot four, needed a bit more room than petite Maddy.

Maddy drove out of the ski-resort parking lot, then down the resort drive. They passed several gorgeous cabins that caught Nelson's attention. Maybe a retreat in an area like this would be nice in the off-season. Some of his teammates had cabins, and he'd been to a couple of them.

Maddy turned onto the main road that would take them

through the quaintness that was Pine Valley, their final destination being the bed and breakfast. A place that felt like Nelson had stepped back in time thirty years.

They passed a book shop, then a realty office.

"Hang on," Nelson said. "There's a café. Think they serve breakfast?"

Maddy's eyes narrowed, and her lips pursed. "That protein shake should last you another good hour."

Nelson threw up his hands. "I'm a two-hundred-and-forty-pound athlete. I need more than a protein shake for breakfast."

Maddy's lips were still pursed.

"Stop the car, Maddy," he said. "I'm getting something hot and full of calories."

She slowed and turned into the handful of parking spots in front of the café.

Nelson put his hand on the door handle. "Want to come?"

"No, thank you."

"I'll be inside if you change your mind," he said, climbing out of the Outback. "Otherwise, I'll walk back to the bed and breakfast."

"You shouldn't walk on concrete," Maddy said, her tone firm. "It's not—"

"I know," Nelson said, leaning back into the car to talk to her. "It's not a natural surface. But my job is to play hockey on hard ice. So walking on concrete could be considered training, right?"

Maddy's lips tightened again.

"I'll take that as a yes." Nelson straightened, then shut the door. Maddy didn't get out. Fine with him. He had to start taking some initiative, or else he'd go bonkers in this small town. He guessed it to be around eight thirty in the morning.

All for You

Since one of Maddy's rules was no phones during training hours, he'd left his in his hotel room.

He'd been in Pine Valley three days now and had yet to eat anything that wasn't green or fibrous or leafy. The Main Street Café had his name all over it. He pushed through the door, trying not to feel guilty about leaving Maddy in the car. Maybe she'd wait for him, maybe not. He didn't mind the walk, and he wouldn't mind the time alone.

The smells hit him like a truck full of goodness. Baking bread, hot coffee, sweet rolls, all rolled into one. It made his brain go a little crazy, and he wondered if the woman at the counter would mind him vaulting over it and scooping about five things into his mouth at once. Instead, he walked to the counter.

"Hi there," he said.

The woman's name tag read *Sarah Lynne*.

"Hello," Sarah Lynne said with a friendly smile as she looked up at him.

Yeah, he was tall, but it seemed the women in this town were short. Starting with Maddy.

"What'll you have?"

It took him only seconds to decide. "Coffee, two of those sweet rolls, and your egg breakfast special with a side of hash browns. And can you double the bacon?"

One of her brows arched as she punched in his order on the register.

After paying, he turned to survey the collection of tables. The smell of the café had been so distracting that he hadn't noticed any of the people. Only one table by the window was occupied by a man and a woman.

The man looked like one of those power-hungry business types. All decked out in a fancy suit. His hair was perfectly styled as if he'd just come from a salon. And the woman sitting across from him wore a slim skirt and pale-colored blouse. Pink? Peach? She also wore some of those incredibly high heels that only few could pull off. They could be used as a weapon if wielded. Her dark hair was pulled into an elegant ponytail, and she was playing with a gold chain at her neck.

And she was crying.

Not sobbing, crying her heart out, but her eyes were rimmed in red, and she clearly looked distressed.

The guy sitting across from her had a hard look in his eyes, as if he was angry or something. Classic jerk.

Maybe it was because Nelson hadn't had a decent meal in days or because he'd been up since 5:00 a.m. enduring nature torture, but he strode over to the table and hauled the fancy-suit man up by the lapels.

Okay, the guy was tall too. And built. But nothing compared to Nelson's sculpted hockey-player build.

"What the hell are you doing?" the guy said, his brown eyes flashing.

"I could ask the same of you," Nelson growled. "Can't you see that the woman is upset? Maybe you should leave her alone."

"Maybe you should leave *us* alone," the man said, his deep voice one of authority.

It seemed he thought he was something special.

Nelson dragged the guy closer until they were almost nose to nose. "Can't do that. I don't like what I'm seeing."

"Hey." The woman was standing now. "Nothing's wrong. Dawson's a friend, and we're having a private conversation."

Without letting go of "Dawson," Nelson turned his head to gaze down at the woman. Up close, he saw that she had the palest of freckles dotted across her nose. Her eyes were a clear blue, and she smelled like some sort of sweet perfume.

"Let go of me," Dawson said. "I'm a lawyer, and you're about two seconds away from getting sued."

Nelson snapped his gaze back to the man. "Of course you're a lawyer. Part of the worst species on earth."

"I'm a lawyer too," the woman said, her voice calm, even. "And Dawson is helping me through a difficult situation. I'm sorry if you thought something else was going on."

Dawson didn't move. Nelson didn't move. Then, slowly, Nelson uncurled his fingers and released the man's suit coat. He stepped back. He looked over at the woman again. Her gaze was open and honest, and although there were still traces of her crying, somehow he believed she wasn't just trying to cover up for a bully of a boyfriend.

"Sorry about that, ma'am," he said, flexing his fingers because all kinds of tension still rippled through him. "It's been a hell of a week."

The woman blinked, and Nelson wondered if she was wearing mascara or if her eyelashes were normally that thick and dark. Of course they'd be dark, because her hair was nearly black...

"I understand," she said. "I've had one of those weeks too. Obviously."

Dawson folded his arms, drawing Nelson's attention again.

"And I apologize to you as well, sir," Nelson continued. "In fact, I'll buy you both your next round of coffee."

Dawson stepped back. "I've got to get to court." He cast a glance at the woman. "Do you want a ride back to the office?"

"No," she said. "I'm going to finish my report, then go hit up the bed and breakfast. Maybe take a nap. I'll move into the office this afternoon."

Nelson frowned. Were they law partners, then? Something more? Not that it was any of his business, and just then, Sarah Lynne called out that his food was ready. As he walked to the counter to fetch it, he overheard Dawson ask the woman if she was sure she didn't want a ride.

She murmured something to him, and by the time Nelson had sat down and arranged his food, the guy had left.

Nelson was starving, but the woman had pulled out a tissue from her purse and wiped at her cheeks.

When she glanced over at him, he realized he'd been staring.

"Sorry," he said. "I should be minding my own business." He picked up the fork and waved it toward the door. "Didn't mean to interfere with you and your boyfriend. I guess I overreacted."

The woman lowered her hand and tilted her head. Her blue eyes scanned him thoroughly. Nelson wondered if he was covered in pine needles and bits of dead leaves. Not to mention some mud. He probably didn't smell too great either.

"I think overreacting is putting it mildly," she said at last.

But Nelson didn't see annoyance in her gaze or hear frustration in her tone of voice. In fact, the edge of her very pretty mouth lifted just slightly.

And her tears seemed to be gone. That was good enough for him.

"Sorry again," Nelson said, and since he'd apologized plenty, it was time to eat. He dug in to the eggs, mixed them into the hash browns, and took his first bite. He chewed and swallowed, then scooped up the next forkful. It seemed there was a little bit of heaven in Pine Valley after all.

Three

The Neanderthal sitting across the café from Lindsey kept stealing glances at her.

Lindsey might be typing up her report on her laptop, but she was aware of every bite he took of his giant-sized breakfast, every sip he took of his coffee, every glance in her direction, and the way his size and personality seemed to fill the entire café.

She'd thought Dawson was a tall, broad-shouldered guy, but this other guy ... this mountain of a man was ... huge. She wondered if he worked for one of those construction crews at the resort. Or maybe he was passing through—or else wouldn't he at least know that Dawson was *the* lawyer in Pine Valley? The two men certainly didn't know each other.

When he'd first entered the café, his mud-caked boots had clomped on the floor, and he hadn't seemed to notice that bits of leaves had fallen from his clothing as he moved to the counter. Lindsey had just finished telling Dawson that she'd decided to file a lawsuit against her old law firm. If she didn't, then she had no doubt that the next female lawyer hired would endure similar harassment.

Lindsey's emotions had been all over the place this past week as she emailed her resignation, cleared out her apartment so she could sublease it, loaded her stuff into a rented van, then drove the two hours to Pine Valley. Dawson already knew most of the story, but he'd wanted to meet for breakfast before the day started to get her the keys to her new office. He'd been a godsend, and she'd just finished spilling out her regrets when Mountain Man had decided to drag Dawson to his feet and pick a fight.

Lindsey had been shocked at first, but then she'd jumped to her feet to defuse the situation. Luckily, both men had backed down immediately. And Lindsey had never felt so . . . protected. No, that wasn't the right word. She didn't know Mountain Man at all. Could only guess at who he was. But apparently all men weren't Paul. Some men were like Dawson. Some men weren't afraid to defend a woman.

And this one man in particular looked as if he could eat a bear for breakfast, if his current meal was any indication.

He looked up from his plate, and their gazes connected. Lindsey realized she'd been staring at Mountain Man for several moments. His eyes were a murky blue, almost a gray color, reminding her of the morning fog back in San Francisco.

She looked away, her skin heating into what could soon become a full blush if she wasn't careful. The guy had one of those strong jaws, his nose was slightly crooked at the top, and his hair . . . Well, the dirty-blond mop on top of his head was somehow sexy, even though she was pretty sure he'd been wearing a beanie before coming into the café.

Lindsey typed out the next paragraph of her report. She was detailing all her experiences at the firm over the last six months. She hoped to finish it today, while everything was fresh in her mind. Dawson had agreed to file the suit for her, and then she hoped to move on, permanently. She didn't know if Pine Valley was where she'd stay forever, but she'd committed to a one-year lease agreement.

It would give her time to get her feet back on the ground. Redefine her goals in life and move forward from the months, and possibly years, of feeling like she was never good enough. That she had to work twice as hard, twice as smart, and twice as long just to prove that she was a good lawyer.

Her eyes burned, and she blinked rapidly. She'd cried enough, and it was time to move on from that too. Lindsey typed out the next paragraph, but she wasn't focusing like she should be. *His* gaze was on her again. She didn't need her peripheral vision to tell her that.

Exhaling slowly, she debated what to do . . . As she saw it, she had three choices. One, introduce herself, two, ignore him, three . . . She couldn't think of a third. A couple of people had come and gone from the café, ordering to-go muffins or coffee. But now, it was just her and Mountain Man. Even the clerk, Sarah Lynne, had gone into the back room for something. Lindsey lifted her gaze again and looked over at Neanderthal.

He didn't look away this time. And neither did she.

"Are you going to be all right?" he asked.

His voice was lower, huskier, than Dawson's. And he was still worried about her. She didn't know what to think about that.

"I'll be fine," she said. "What about you?"

One of his brows lifted a fraction, but he didn't answer. He seemed to be too busy studying her.

"You said you'd had a hell of a week," she prompted.

His brow relaxed. "Yeah. I'm in some intense physical therapy for an injury, which apparently includes a diet plan of eating like a squirrel."

She scanned him and tried to remember if he'd appeared injured or lame at any point in time. No, she decided. "What happened?"

He hesitated.

Now he was reluctant to talk?

"I mean, from my viewpoint, you don't look all that injured," Lindsey said. "You trudged in here, then stormed over and nearly got into a fistfight."

He didn't look chagrined, at all. "My knee. Grade-one medial collateral ligament sprain. Sounds worse than it is. And I have a claustrophobia problem. Found that out in the MRI."

This guy was not afraid to share information. "So you're in physical therapy but still tried to take on Dawson Harris?"

He shrugged. "I don't always make the best decisions. All I know is that it's been a pain in the as—uh, *rear end*—dealing with this injury."

Lindsey shut the lid of her laptop. Did he just correct his language? "Trying to cut back on swearing?"

"I am." His eyes had lightened a shade, from a dark fog to more of a morning mist.

She couldn't believe that she felt like laughing. It had been a long time. She had the sudden urge to tease him. "Because you're around ladies?"

He glanced over at the counter, where Sarah Lynne was rearranging the muffins and donuts. Then he rose, and with Lindsey still sitting, he seemed even taller than she remembered. She watched as he trudged over in those boots, and well, she couldn't help notice how nicely his faded jeans fit. He sat at the table next to hers, which put him in much closer proximity.

"Here's the thing," he said in a lowered voice, his gray eyes trained on hers. "I'm trying to cut out all the negative words for a couple of weeks. Part of the holistic healing process, you know. At least that's what Maddy tells me."

"Your holistic trainer?"

"The very one."

The fact that this hulk of a guy would listen to anyone was quite amusing. "So you can't swear?"

"No."

"Or say anything negative?"

"Well . . . not about myself," he said.

"But if you saw an upset woman, you'd take action despite your injury?"

His mouth twitched.

She almost smiled.

"I'm Nelson," he said, extending his hand.

She looked at his large hand, sighed, then put her hand in his. They slowly shook. "Lindsey Gerber. Do you have a last name, Nelson?"

"I go by my last name." He still hadn't released her hand.

And she found she didn't mind. His hand was large, warm, strong, but gentle too. "What's your first name?"

"Tyler," he said. "Or Ty. Everyone calls me Nelson, though."

"Okay, Nelson," she said. They should probably release hands. "I go by Lindsey. Not Lind. Not Lin. And definitely not Gerber."

He smiled then, and Lindsey was glad she was sitting down. His smile had probably melted hearts. Not hers, of course, but definitely other women's hearts.

"I like *Lindsey* the best out of those choices, so don't worry," he said.

"Why would I be worried?" she asked, drawing her hand away from his.

"Because we'll probably cross paths again, since we're staying at the same bed and breakfast."

That debunked her view of him as a construction worker. "You don't live here?"

"Nope. I'm on a pseudo physical therapy holistic-and-all-natural wilderness retreat."

He'd stated it so matter-of-factly, yet it sounded . . . strange. She felt like smiling. "I've never heard of that . . . what did you call it?"

"Pseudo—"

She put her hand on his arm, because they were sitting close enough to touch. "It's okay, you don't have to repeat it."

His lips twitched. "Good."

She smiled. Then laughed.

He watched her, amusement sparking in those gray eyes of his.

And . . . her hand was still on his arm, where all she felt was solid muscle beneath her fingers. Who was this guy?

She really should stop touching him. "So how did you get injured, Nelson?" Was she really chatting up this guy, *Nelson*? Who went by their last name anyway?

"Someone crashed into me," he said. "Hurt like a son of a b-beast."

"Oh, wow," she said. "Was the other guy okay?"

"Skated away just fine," he said. "Didn't even look back."

Lindsey frowned. "Skated?"

"Hockey game," he said. "I play for the Falcons. We were up against the Seattle Blacks last week, and—"

Several things clicked into place in Lindsey's mind. "Wait. You're a pro hockey player?" She might be more apt to watch baseball, because, well, baseball players . . . but if Nelson was a pro hockey player, that explained so much. The body. The intensity of his gaze. The in-your-face personality. The . . .

"Yeah. I'm a goaltender."

Okay, so from whatever little hockey Lindsey had seen—which amounted to part of the Stanley Cup if she happened to be at a sports grill—she knew the goaltender was the most important player on the team. And they got tons of action. Hit a lot too.

"Are you having a conversation in your head?" he asked in that low tone of his.

Nelson . . . *Tyler* Nelson . . . Lindsey was most definitely going to google this guy. It was kind of cool to meet a pro athlete—albeit an injured one. Although, looking at him, she had no doubt he'd recover just fine. He was built like an ox. In fact, the more she studied him, the more things she noticed. His nose must have been broken at least once. That explained the crooked part of his nose—which did nothing to take away from his handsomeness. And there was a scar at his temple, and another, smaller one below his lip. And . . .

"Uh, Lindsey, are you okay?" He leaned close.

Oh boy. He smelled like pine trees and rain. Which pretty much went perfectly with his murky eyes.

"I'm okay," she said. "Why?"

His lips curved, but his gaze searched hers. "You sort of checked out for a couple of minutes."

She blinked. "I did, didn't I?" She leaned back in her chair to put a little more distance between them. Not that she wanted to, but she could think more clearly if she wasn't noticing how his open collar revealed the base of his throat. Which was tanned just like the rest of him. He had to be from someplace warmer than Pine Valley.

"Sorry. Don't be offended. I used to check out like that all the time in school," she said. "Had to work like crazy to stay attentive in law school since we were graded on lectures and not necessarily textbooks."

"Maybe you have ADD?" he said.

Tyler Nelson was probably the most unique person she'd ever spoken to. "You know something about ADD?"

He lifted one of his thick shoulders. "My little sister has it."

Four

Nelson tried to answer the questions that Lindsey Gerber asked about his sister's ADD. How they had gotten on this topic was a mystery to him, but he'd go with it. This woman had no idea who he was, and that was refreshing. And she wasn't intimidated by his size, another bonus in his book. Of course, her "friend" had been a good-sized guy himself. He wondered how far their friendship status went.

Not that it was any of Nelson's business. Hel—er—heck, he wasn't in Pine Valley to meet women. So he should probably be a good patient and head back to the bed and breakfast, where Maddy was sure to be waiting for him, to lead him through a round of Pilates or something.

But he was really wondering what sort of perfume Lindsey Gerber wore, because he definitely liked the mellow, sweet smell. He also wanted to ask her how the *heck* she walked in those high heels of hers.

"How old is Becca?" Lindsey asked.

Oh, yeah, they were talking about his sister. "Twenty-six, or maybe twenty-seven . . . It's just us since our mom passed away a few years ago." His voice trailed off, and he cleared his throat. His mom had been his biggest supporter, but cancer had done its damage. He really wanted to change the subject, but would it be rude? Besides, he wanted to know more about Lindsey. Or would it be too obvious that he was sort of . . . well, interested in her. Not interested like asking her out, but intrigued. Maybe it was because he was away from his usual routine and feeling out of sorts with the injury and everything?

Someone came into the café, and Nelson waited until they went to the counter, then he said, "Can I ask you a personal question?"

Her dark brows lifted, and her clear blue eyes focused on him. "Sure, I guess."

"What kind of perfume are you wearing?"

He hadn't expected her to flinch, then gather up her things as if she was going to leave.

"Um, did I say something wrong?" he asked. When she didn't answer, but shoved a notebook and her laptop into a bag on the other side of her chair, he said, "If that was way too personal, then forget I asked. I was just curious, but I'll understand if you want to keep your secrets."

She turned to face him then, her cheeks an angry pink. "I'm not interested, Tyler Nelson. Not in you, or any other hunk of a man who happens to walk through that door."

He had no reply but only stared as she rose to her feet.

"We're finished here," she continued, keeping her voice low, but Nelson had no doubt that the handful of people in the café could hear every single word. "Please don't try to talk to me again, even if you see me."

Nelson pushed to his feet, and he guessed her to be about

five foot eight without those heels of hers. With them on, she was nearly six feet. Which meant he still had a good five inches on her. "Look, I'm sorry. Believe me, I didn't mean—"

She moved past him, her arm brushing against his, and he stepped back to give her more room. It was a strange thing to watch her walk out of the café. A woman whom he'd barely met and had apologized to at least a dozen times.

Nelson could feel the stares at his back, or were they *glares*? He was the outsider here, the interloper in Pine Valley. And he should probably make himself scarce. So he pulled out his wallet and left a five-dollar bill on the table. He left the café and found that Lindsey Gerber hadn't made it too far down the street. Those heels couldn't be the fastest transportation. And his da—dang knee was starting to act up.

So Nelson slowed his step, since he was going in the same direction as Lindsey and he didn't want her to think he was following her. She reached a corner, and good thing she didn't turn around, because who knew what she'd do if she saw him a half block behind. Maybe she'd put those high heels to good use.

As Nelson walked, he reviewed their entire conversation in his mind. She hadn't seemed bothered by any of their bantering until he asked about her perfume. Maybe . . . he stopped as he reached the corner and waited for a car to pass. Maybe she thought he was coming onto her? That might explain it. Maybe she had a boyfriend—that Dawson guy—or she was one of those women who despised men. Nelson had met his share. But that didn't explain her friendliness earlier, which had bordered on flirting.

Nelson blew out a breath of frustration. He should probably ask his sister if there was some unwritten conversation code between men and women wherein the man didn't ask certain questions. But if he did ask Becca such a question, she'd smell his motivations a mile away ... or six hundred miles to be exact, since she lived in Portland. The bigger question was, *did* he have motivations? Had he been coming onto Lindsey Gerber?

Sure, she was beautiful. Easy to talk to ... until ... But truth be told, she wasn't really his type. He dated women who hung around the hockey arena. Women who were peppy, full of questions, laughing—giggling to be exact—at every word that fell from his mouth. Being a pro athlete sure made it easy to get a date. Of course the fact that he was twenty-nine and hadn't been serious with anyone, unless he counted dating Suzanne his senior year in high school for an entire six months, probably indicated that he wasn't the serious-relationship type.

Yep. That was his record.

Usually, he'd go out with a woman about three times, maybe four, before his interest waned. Maybe he was the one with ADD. Was it possible to have relationship ADD?

Lindsey was almost to the bed and breakfast, and he once again slowed his step as she entered the building. He wondered which room she was in. Maybe his same floor? Then he couldn't help but run into her. What would she do then?

Nelson decided to walk around the place and go in through the back door. Less chance of running into Maddy that way, because there was a good chance she'd be waiting in the small lobby for him. Not that he was avoiding his next phase of therapy ... but he thought he'd at least shoot his sister a text.

Once inside his room, he turned on his phone. Dozens of texts piled in, followed by several chimes indicating emails as well. He opened the first text strand, the one from the team. Coach had sent out the instructions, which amounted to a team meeting followed by a light workout that morning, because there was a game tonight. A game Nelson would be missing and Ben would be playing goaltender in.

Nelson closed out the text strand before his mind went into that dark rabbit hole, and he opened up the next text—from his sister. Convenient. She was being rather sweet since his injury and texted him once or twice a day for updates.

Hiked like a billy goat today, he texted her back. *Finally got some decent food in me. But I think I pissed off a lawyer. Two, in fact.*

Becca must have been on her phone, because she replied right back. *Wait. What? I thought you were in the sticks.*

Me too, Nelson wrote. *Pine Valley has just enough people who need lawyers. They'll probably sue because they have nothing else to do.*

Becca sent back a laughing-face emoji. *Want me to come visit? We could paint the town. You know, show them how the Nelsons have fun.*

Nelson scoffed. *I don't know what you're talking about, little sister. Besides, don't you have some Barbies to play with or something?*

That's right, big, tough brother, she wrote. *I'm the one with the college degree, while you insist on chasing around a three-inch hockey puck every week.*

He chuckled. His sister knew how to throw down; it was kind of their thing. He crossed to the window that looked out into a wooded area. This town was full of pine trees. It wasn't too hard to see where the name Pine Valley came from. *When I'm retired in ten years and living the good life, you'll still be paying off your student loans.*

Who says I haven't paid them off yet? She wrote. *Have you checked your money market account lately?*

You wouldn't dare.

Becca typed back the angel emoji.

Yes, Becca was his financial planner. Made perfect sense when she got her business management degree followed by an MBA. Nelson wasn't worried about his sister's access to his accounts. She was the biggest tightwad he'd ever met. Well, except for him. She still wore sweats from her freshman year—in high school. Impressive.

Pretty much anything decent she owned, Nelson had bought her.

Another text buzzed on his phone. From Maddy. *Pilates in 15.*

Ah. There it was. He typed back. *Okay.* Because really, there was no other choice. Coach had already drilled that into him. Nelson had to finish every bit of this program, or his position might be in jeopardy. Things with his team had been rocky the past year or so. Nelson felt like he only had two friends on the team, and not that he was looking for friendships among his teammates, but respect had been pretty thin too. He pulled his mind from that rabbit hole too.

Hey, got a question, he wrote to Becca. *I can't explain much because I'm due for another torture session. But is it okay for a man to ask a woman what kind of perfume she's wearing? I mean, in a way that's not offensive?*

His phone rang. Becca was calling.

"Is the answer really that complicated?" he asked his sister.

"I need context," she said, laughter in her voice.

"I don't have time," he said. "Maddy's waiting for me, and I need to shower first to thaw my frozen feet. You should see my boots, they're covered in—"

"Ty," his sister cut in. She was the only who called him that. "Context, or I can't help you. And I'm assuming you want help, or else you wouldn't have asked me."

Nelson hesitated. Then he sat in the rocking chair—yep,

there was a rocking chair in his room—and it creaked as if offended. "One of those lawyers I mentioned?"

"Yeah?"

"Well, one was a woman," he said. "You know the type. All businesslike. Fancy suit. Opinionated. Wearing those high heels that have no right being counted as footwear."

"Stilettos?" Becca's voice sounded very, very amused.

"Yeah, whatever," he said. "Long story short, because I really do have to go, I asked Lindsey what kind of perfume she was wearing. Because, you know, she smelled nice, and the more we talked, the more I wondered. So I didn't see any harm in asking. But she about took my head off for one simple question."

Becca didn't say anything.

He heard a rustling sound, or was it scoffing? Whatever it was, it was a bit muffled. "Um, are you still there?"

"I'm here."

She was . . . laughing. So hard that it sounded like she was having trouble breathing.

"Should I call 9-1-1?" he deadpanned. "Maybe you need a breathing treatment?"

She wheezed, then started laughing again.

Nelson closed his eyes. "You're not helping. At. All. I'm hanging up in five seconds if you don't tell me what I f-freaking did wrong."

"I'm sorry," she gasped. "I'm really, really sorry."

She didn't sound sorry.

"I . . . I can't get over the image of you asking a woman about her perfume. I mean, if I didn't know you better, I'd think you were—"

"Seriously, Becca?" he cut in. "*Three* seconds."

"Okay, okay." She took a great gulp of air. "I think it's kind of . . . sweet. But apparently, she thought you were trying to pick up on her or something."

He knew it. He didn't need to ask his sister after all. He should have just gone with his gut. She was having way too much fun with this.

"What did she say?" she asked, obviously using a great deal of control to form her words.

Well, Nelson had already come this far. "We were having a totally normal conversation until I asked her. Then she got mad and told me not to speak to her again. Which normally wouldn't be a problem, but we're staying at the same bed and breakfast."

When Becca went quiet again, she wasn't laughing.

"Sis?"

"Um, she sounds like she has some issues."

"*Issues*?" Nelson asked. "Like what?"

Becca released a sigh. "I don't know. You'd have to ask her. Which isn't going to happen by the sound of it. But I think she's been jaded, or she's been jilted, or whatever."

"Another guy?"

"Yeah, but there's probably more to the story," she said. "Women in her profession, heck, in any high-profile profession, get a lot of crap. Mostly from men. Coming onto them. She probably thought you were just another jerk trying to pick her up."

Nelson was the one who went quiet this time. And he couldn't believe he was about to ask his sister this . . . "What if I *did* want to, uh, get to know her better?"

"I think this one's out of your league, bro," she said. "Sorry to give you the bad news. But for your sake, you should respect her wishes. You know, take the rejection like a man and move on."

"Huh," Nelson said. "But what if—"

"Ty," Becca cut in. "Unless *she* approaches *you* or talks to you first, respect *her* wishes. That's all I can tell you.

Anything you try will just backfire. Remember, she's a lawyer, and I'm pretty sure that not even you could charm a woman like her who's made up her mind."

"Of course I'll respect her wishes," Nelson said. "I just don't know why women have to be such a mystery."

"Maybe I will come to Pine Valley," Becca said. "If only to catch a glimpse of the woman who's befuddled my big, tough brother."

"Funny," Nelson said. "I'm curious, that's all. Nothing more. I mean, I met her like an hour ago, and we only talked for about twenty minutes. So there's no befuddlement going on here."

"Uh-huh," Becca mused.

Three minutes later, Nelson had hung up with Becca, nowhere nearer understanding what had set Lindsey off. Yeah, so maybe it was a little flirtatious to ask her about her perfume, but it was also a simple question. Completely innocent. It wasn't like he was interested in a woman like Lindsey. All sophisticated, long legs, sharp tongue, blue, blue eyes, and heels that could impale a man's heart.

Five

Lindsey really should have taken Dawson up on his offer to help her move into the office. He said he'd be done with court that afternoon, but like the stubborn person she was, she'd been carrying in file boxes one at a time into her newly leased office space. She'd been at it for two hours, and she was sweaty, tired, and grumpy.

Her breakfast had long since worn off, and her feet killed. Yeah, she'd changed out of her suit and heels into some jeans and tennis shoes. Good thing, because her T-shirt was dirty, and she'd snagged her jeans on a low protruding nail on the wall and ripped a small hole. She didn't know why in the world there was a nail that low on the wall, but Dawson wasn't here to ask.

She peeked into his office. It was neat and orderly, much like Dawson himself. Lindsey prided herself in being organized too, but her emotions were all over the place, to say the least. Case in point . . . when she'd practically taken off

Tyler Nelson's head at the café. He'd asked her about her perfume, and... something inside her snapped. Hard. She knew Nelson wasn't like Paul or other jerks she'd met. It had been fun to talk to Mr. Pro Hockey Player. He'd been quite entertaining. And yeah, she'd gotten the vibe that he was checking her out. But not a creepy vibe.

So why had she freaked out?

Well, she knew why. Paul's antics and threats had made her overly defensive. And that last week hadn't been easy. Still, she could keep her cool in a courtroom full of witnesses and jury members who were analyzing her every move. Yet a handful of hours ago, she'd lost it.

Lindsey walked out of the office building, which was a renovated old house that Dawson had told her was built in the thirties. The place was quaint, and it was obvious that Dawson had put a lot of thought into the renovations. The road was set back a street from Main Street, and on one side of the lawyer office was a dental complex, and on the other side, another renovated house that advertised massages. Which sounded pretty good right now.

She headed to the van, which she'd parked backwards in front of the building so that she could unload it easier. She estimated that she was about half done with the unloading, and even though it was a cool day, she'd nearly drunk down two water bottles. She took another guzzle of water before reaching for another box. As she turned toward the building, a couple of bike riders came into view.

She glanced over to see that they were a man and woman ... the broad shoulders and dark-blond hair of the man reminded her of ... Nelson.

Lindsey's shoe caught on the first step leading to the porch. She pitched forward, the box still in her hands, and she had the good sense to release the box so that she could catch herself against the steps. At least she hadn't hit her face, but her palms and knees scraped against the concrete. Her knees were, of course, protected mostly by her jeans, but the sting in her hands was immediate.

What were the chances?

And . . . here it came.

"Are you all right?" the woman asked.

"Lindsey?" the man said. Nelson's voice.

"You know her?" the woman continued.

"We, uh, met at the café this morning," Nelson continued.

Lindsey had yet to turn around from her fallen state on the steps. She blinked against the stinging of her eyes because, yes, her hands hurt that bad. She steeled her emotions. Apparently this day *could* get worse. She rotated until she was sitting on the steps, and the woman had already reached her and placed a hand on her shoulder.

"That was quite the fall," the woman said, crouching down and peering at her with hazel eyes. "What happened?"

"I just tripped, that's all," Lindsey said, finding her voice to be surprisingly steady.

"I'm Maddy. Hardy," the woman said in a clear, singsong voice, as if she were trying to soothe an upset child. "And you're Lindsey, right?"

"Right," Lindsey said.

"Do you know how old you are, Lindsey?" Maddy asked.

Lindsey blinked. "Uh, twenty-eight, but what does—"

"Very good, Lindsey," Maddy said. "Now tell me how many fingers I'm holding up."

The woman was about forty, Lindsey guessed, and looked like she was a marathon runner with the spandex shorts and top she wore. Or maybe she was another pro athlete and raced bikes?

"Maddy," Nelson cut in. "I've got it."

He sat next to Lindsey on the steps and drew one of her hands toward him, then poured water from a bottle onto her scraped palms. The cold water was a shock for a couple of seconds, then it started to soothe.

"Let me see your other hand," Nelson said, releasing her first hand.

She lifted her other hand, and he proceeded to pour more water on.

"Do you have a first-aid kit in that van?" he asked.

"Um, I don't think so," Lindsey said. She'd chewed out this man a few hours ago, but now here he was helping her. "It's a rental."

"Why don't you check inside the building, Maddy," Nelson said. "Look in the bathroom."

The woman moved past them and headed up the steps.

Now that he'd stopped pouring water on her hands, angry red scrapes started to burn again.

"You banged up your knees pretty good too," Nelson said.

It was then that Lindsey noticed that she'd ripped holes in the knees of her jeans. Her knees were throbbing, but her hands hurt more right now.

"Hope these aren't expensive designer jeans," he said, even though she had yet to speak a word to him. "Unless you're into the ripped-knee look."

She shook her head. What was wrong with her? She'd tripped on a few stairs, and now she was apparently a helpless damsel.

"Only found some hand sanitizer," Maddy said, coming out of the offices. "But that will only burn her scrapes."

Nelson looked over at Maddy. "Agreed. How close is the nearest store?"

Maddy placed her hands on her hips. "A couple of blocks. I could head over on the bike and be back in a jiffy."

They were having this entire conversation without her.

Before she knew it, Maddy had climbed on her bike and rode away.

"How do you feel?" Nelson asked. "Do you want something to drink?"

She nodded again, mute.

He rose and crossed to his bike, where he must have gotten the first water bottle he used on her hands.

She couldn't help but notice that while he wasn't wearing biker's spandex, his shorts and fitted T-shirt made it no secret that he was a man who probably had less than 2 percent fat on his body. He also wore some sort of neoprene brace on his left knee. He unstrapped a water bottle, then walked back to her.

She averted her gaze because she shouldn't be checking out Tyler Nelson; besides, she was sure she looked a mess. In a lot of ways. Inside and out.

He didn't sit by her again but handed over the water bottle after unscrewing the lid.

She took a drink, then handed it back. "Thanks," she said, finally speaking. "You really don't have to patch me up. I'll be fine in a few minutes."

"It's not a problem," Nelson said.

His gaze wasn't leaving her face, and she brushed back some stray hair from her face with the tips of her fingers. She took a breath. "And I'm sorry . . . for earlier." She should probably explain why she'd been so snappish, but now wasn't the time. Besides, moving to Pine Valley was about putting the misery of the past six months behind her.

"I didn't mean to upset you." He moved to pick up the books that had tumbled out of the box.

"You really don't have to clean up," she said, rising to her feet. She winced at the sharp ache in her knees.

Nelson was at her side in an instant, grasping her elbow. "Easy."

"I'm okay," she said. "Just sore."

He was standing really close to her, and although it was clear he'd been exercising plenty on the bike, he still smelled of the outdoors, spice, and pine.

His deep-gray eyes scanned her face. "You didn't hit your head, did you?" he asked.

"No."

He didn't move for a moment, and she didn't tell him to step back.

Then he released her arm. "How about you tell me where to put these boxes?"

She stared as he hefted the box from the ground. "What about your knee?"

He started up the steps. No tripping for him. "I can carry a few boxes. If you have a piano to move, then I might have to pass."

She followed him up the steps, then opened the door for him so he could enter the building. "My office is the one on the right. I'm lining the boxes of books by the wall for now until I get a bookcase in there."

Nelson continued into the office space and set the box over by the wall she pointed to. Then he headed outside again. She followed. Her hands might be scraped, but she could still carry boxes.

"I've got it," Nelson said, when she joined him at the van. "Please. It's really no trouble. All I have planned for the rest of the day is trying to talk Maddy into giving me a couple of hours off to watch my team play tonight."

Lindsey watched him heft another box, one she knew was quite heavy. His arms were plenty strong, but adding weight when his knee was injured might not be so smart. She pulled her gaze away from the way his shoulders and biceps defined his T-shirt.

"Are you sure this is okay with your knee?" she asked.

His gray eyes cut to her, and one edge of his mouth lifted. "If it starts hurting, I'll stop."

Lindsey stepped to the side so that he could pass. She watched him head into the building again. The more Nelson helped her out, the worse she felt for getting angry with him. But she had to admit that the help was nice. She was apparently more out of shape than she'd realized. Maybe the slower life in Pine Valley would give her some time to get into a regular exercise routine.

Nelson returned, and for the next few minutes, Lindsey stood around while he carried in box after box. There were only a couple left when Maddy arrived on her bike, a grocery sack dangling from one of her bike handles.

"Got some Neosporin and Band-Aids," Maddy said.

So while Nelson emptied the van of the last few things, Maddy tended to Lindsey while they sat on the edge of the porch. "This should heal pretty quickly," Maddy said. "Now, how do you know Nelson?"

"I—I don't really," Lindsey said. He was inside the building at the moment. "We crossed paths at the café this morning."

Maddy nodded. "I know about him eating at the café. He needs to eat whole foods only, especially during his recovery. Speeds up the healing process."

Lindsey wondered if a man the size of Nelson would be satisfied with whole foods. She guessed the answer was no. "Are you a nutritionist too?"

"Not licensed, if that's what you're asking," Maddy said. "But I've read plenty of books."

Sounded so *not* official.

"You've done enough here, Nelson," Maddy said. "You owe me three more miles on the bike, then an ice down."

Lindsey snapped her gaze to Nelson. He didn't seem bothered by Maddy's commanding tone, nor did he move away from the van. He knelt on the back to shift the rear bench into place.

Maddy clicked her tongue. "If he reinjures that knee, his coach will fire me."

"He said he wasn't hurting."

Maddy scoffed. "Is that what he told you?"

"Um, yes," she said. "Or I wouldn't have let him carry boxes."

"He's hurting all right," Maddy said. "And he's a very stubborn man." She left Lindsey's side and crossed to Nelson as he backed out of the van.

"Come on, we're not done for the day," Maddy said.

Nelson straightened and brushed off his hands. "Yes, ma'am."

When Maddy turned away, the slightest grimace passed over his face. Lindsey's heart sank. What if he really had overdone it? Yet he was out riding a bike, so she wasn't sure what was or wasn't okay with his therapy.

He joined Maddy at the bikes, then he climbed on. Before he rode away, he looked over at Lindsey. "Game's at seven thirty if you're interested."

Before she could answer or ask him any questions, he fixed his feet to the pedals and headed after Maddy, who had a good start.

Lindsey watched Nelson until he rounded the corner down the street. He'd come out of nowhere, it seemed, but he was suddenly everywhere. Now, with the entire van unloaded, thanks to Tyler Nelson, she'd have time to finish that report.

Six

The bed and breakfast was quiet as Nelson headed into the back-lobby-slash-game-room, where the only television in the place was located. He carried an ice pack for his throbbing knee and his ever-present water bottle. He located the remote and settled onto the large couch. The place was decorated like a bear haven, with small wood bear statues lining a shelf on the wall and a few bear paintings on the wall.

Nelson found the sports channel just as the announcers read the starting lineup for the Falcons. Nelson tried not to let it bother him that his name wasn't read. The announcer mentioned that he was still out with a knee injury. He clenched his jaw as the announcer speculated on when he might return. "Six weeks at the most," the guy said.

"Try three weeks," Nelson said to the television. He arranged the ice bag on his knee, and the cold began to immediately penetrate. The first minute or so was always the most uncomfortable, but then things would go numb.

The emptiness of the place made him assume that most of the guests had checked out, save for Lindsey Gerber. He was feeling pretty good about the peace they'd made. Maybe the next time they ran into each other, she wouldn't avoid him. So he guessed it was lucky they'd passed by her new office when they did. He'd tried not to check her out, or at least not be obvious about it.

But he was human, male, and well . . . human. Lindsey Gerber was a beautiful woman. Both when she was decked out in those high heels of hers and when she was wearing simple jeans and tennis shoes. He'd noticed at the café she didn't wear any sort of a wedding ring, but he had yet to learn if she was in a serious relationship. With Dawson or some other guy. If she was, then there was no chance she'd be showing up tonight to watch the game. Well, she might not anyway. She hadn't even said she liked hockey.

And . . . he should probably pay attention to the game, because Ben had just made an amazing save.

Nelson wanted to be happy for Ben, but he only felt mad at himself all over again. Sitting around in Pine Valley with an ice pack on his knee wasn't his first choice.

He took an obligatory drink from his water bottle, hoping that Maddy would be happy wherever she was or whatever she was doing. What *did* she do at night? Did she really go to bed at 8:00 p.m. when she usually told him it was time to call it a night? Maybe she had a secret night life. He chuckled at the thought. No, Maddy probably went on a midnight run.

"Watch out on the left!" Nelson said to the television. "Come on, Minky, keep your eyes open!"

But Minky collided with a Denver Charger, and his shot went wild. Minky recovered the puck quickly, then shot again. The Chargers' goaltender deftly blocked the shot, then sent the puck skimming past the half line. Once again, a Charger took control of the puck and took the straight shot to the goal.

Ben moved, blocking the puck, but then his skate slipped at the last second, and the puck crossed the goal line.

"No!" Nelson groaned and dropped his head. Only four minutes into the game, and already the Chargers were up by one.

"Everything okay?" a woman's voice asked from across the room.

Nelson looked up to see Linsey Gerber. "The Chargers just scored, which isn't my team," he said, and even though the disappointment of the goal stabbed through him, he felt insanely happy that Lindsey Gerber was standing twenty feet away.

"Right, you play for the Falcons."

She stood in the entryway that led to the main hall. The woman changed more in one day than most people did in a week. Gone were the ripped jeans and T-shirt, and now she wore printed leggings that were quite ... fitted, as leggings were. But he tried not to notice how her black V-neck top hugged her hips and followed her rather nice curves. The look on her face told him that she was wondering if she'd made the right choice ... to come watch the game with him? Nelson didn't know if he was jumping to conclusions, but a guy could only hope that her appearance meant that she didn't have a boyfriend and was keeping her options open.

If Becca could hear his thoughts, she'd have a good laugh.

Nelson lifted the ice pack from his knee and shifted over on the couch, since he was sitting dead center. He made it a point not to grimace at the movement despite the soreness. And no, he wasn't sore from carrying boxes of books; it was from the biking. Or maybe the Pilates. Or quite possibly the hiking that morning.

"Have a seat," he said. "There's plenty of room."

Lindsey looked like she was ready to bolt at any second, so he redirected his gaze to the television, hoping that maybe his nonchalance would draw her a little farther into the room.

His peripheral vision told him he was right.

She walked into the room but still didn't sit down.

"Don't do it, Ben," Nelson said to the television. The goaltender had moved too far forward. "Move back. Haven't you already learned your lesson?"

He sighed and leaned back against the couch. Still Lindsey hadn't joined him.

"Is Ben the goaltender when you're not playing?" she asked.

"Yeah." Nelson glanced over at her, hiding a smile that she was still hanging out in the room. "He's a good guy, but man, he makes small mistakes that cost us in the long run."

Lindsey folded her arms. "Like coming out too far from the goal box?"

She'd pulled her long, dark hair back into one of those messy buns his sister seemed to favor. On Lindsey, it only exposed her slim neck and drew attention to her collarbones. He wondered if she was still wearing that perfume.

"Yeah," he said. "Do you watch hockey?"

Lindsey moved a little closer to the couch but still didn't sit. Should he shift to the far side? Would that make her more comfortable?

"I've, uh, seen parts of the Stanley Cup." Her gaze moved from him to the television.

"Parts?"

"You know, at a sports grill or maybe when it's been on at a friend's house."

He nodded. "Yeah, I get it. Hockey's not the most popular American sport like baseball or football."

"Well, I don't *hate* hockey," she said.

He smiled. "Then sit down. You're making me antsy."

One of her brows raised, but he detected the smallest bit of softening in her expression.

"Go the *other* way, Minky," Nelson grumbled. But his annoyance at the starting forward of his team was greatly tempered when Lindsey sat at the other end of the couch. About as far away as she could get without sitting on the armrest. Still, it was progress.

"How's the knee?" she asked.

He hated that question, but coming from her, spoken in a concerned tone, it wasn't all that bad. "Every day's better."

"You didn't hurt it moving the boxes, did you?"

Nelson turned his head. Her eyes were a darker blue in the lamplight of the room. And things were too dim to see her freckles. "Moving boxes felt like a vacation compared to what Maddy's having me do. Although I can't complain. Or *shouldn't* complain."

"Because that would be too much negativity?" The edges of her mouth lifted.

"Exactly," he said with a chuckle. "Gotta think the good thoughts. Keep drinking barrels of water. And not let it bother me when Ben gets scored on."

She smiled. He didn't know what he'd said to deserve that smile, but he wanted to find a way to duplicate it. Over and over.

"Not a fan of water?" she asked.

"Water's essential, we all know that, but I think I drink more water than the entire da—darned country of Nepal."

She was still smiling. "I'm sure Maddy knows what she's doing. She told me she reads a lot of books on nutrition."

"There you go," Nelson said with a shrug. "She's learning

from the experts. My life and my stomach are absolutely fine in her hands."

Lindsey laughed.

Nelson was pretty sure his heart flipped over, even though he knew it wasn't scientifically or physically possible.

She slipped off her shoes—no high heels tonight—and tucked her feet up on the couch.

So . . . she was going to stay awhile.

Despite hockey being his life and love, it was hard to tear his gaze from the woman on the other side of the couch and pay attention to the game. Because that was why he was sitting in front of the television—to watch the game—right?

He forced his eyes back to the television. "Come on, Minky," Nelson muttered, watching the forward make a play for the goal again. Minky shot, and it was blocked at the last minute by the Chargers' goaltender.

Nelson blew out a breath. The Chargers were in control now and definitely dominating the entire game. Minky tried to cut off one of the Chargers, and the other player turned and drove an elbow into Minky's side.

The two men crashed against the wall, and Nelson shot to his feet. "Get off him! Ref, do something!"

Nelson immediately regretted his swift action because his knee was so numb that he nearly lost his balance. "Whoa," he said, grabbing for the couch. "Dammit."

Lindsey jumped to her feet and grasped his arm. "Are you okay?"

Nelson closed his eyes for a second, because stars were twinkling at the edge of his vision. "I'm okay. Just stood up too fast. This blasted knee is like a block of ice right now, thanks to Maddy's insistence that I ice the hel—heck out of it every night."

Lindsey was still holding onto his arm. And she smelled

of her mystery perfume again. He couldn't have planned this better. But of course, the second that thought crossed his mind, she released him and stepped back.

"Well, take it easy, Nelson," she said. "It's only a game."

He snapped his gaze to her.

Lindsey smiled.

She was teasing, that he could see now, but still, those were fighting words. Resting her hands on her hips, she looked him up and down. What was she trying to do, make him blush? Not that he ever blushed—he was a pro hockey player, after all.

"Do you always get this wound up watching a game?" she asked, her hands still on those curvy hips of hers.

"Uh . . ." How did he answer that?

"I mean, I think it's cool that our society idolizes athletes enough to facilitate entire careers and events based around such a sporting event, but in the end . . . it's chasing a ball around, or a *puck*, in this case. Not exactly a life-or-death occasion."

He blinked. "Is that lawyer speak or something? Because I'm hoping you're not insulting my entire existence up to this point. And what will continue to be my life for, oh, possibly until my death, because I plan on coaching after I retire from the game."

One of her brows raised. "How long have you been playing?"

"My dad took me on the ice when I was six years old," he said. "Haven't looked back since. Kept me out of trouble in high school and paid for my college."

She seemed even more surprised at this. "College, huh?"

He took a step closer, even though he really wanted to sit and give his knee a rest. "You thought I was an uneducated blockhead?"

Her mouth twitched. Nelson was pretty sure she'd put on lip gloss before coming into the game room.

"What did you study?" she asked, her voice softer now.

"Sports psychology."

"Really?"

"Really."

She nodded and lowered her hands. Then she moved back and sat on the couch. *Not* at the very end, but more toward the middle.

Nelson retook his seat in the same spot, which only put him about a foot and a half away from Lindsey. The fight had apparently been cleaned up, and Minky was back on the ice, no worse for the wear.

Nelson repositioned the ice bag on his knee.

"Gardenia," Lindsey said in a quiet voice.

He looked over at her. "Garden-*what*?"

Her blue eyes met his. "That's the name of my perfume."

Seven

Today was the day, Lindsey decided. The beginning of her new life. She'd returned the rental van the day before, and today would be her first real day in the office. So she was going to start it off right by running this morning, then after showering, she'd head to the Main Street Café. Start to mingle with the locals.

She needed to start drumming up clients, although Dawson said he had plenty of leads for her.

Lindsey climbed out of bed, and after brushing her teeth, she pulled her hair into a tight ponytail. Then she dressed in very outdated running clothes, but who'd see her? She slipped her cell phone into her jacket pocket because the March mornings had been fairly cool, and there was still snow clinging to the slopes.

Which Tyler Nelson had told her about in great detail, since apparently he hiked them every morning. The thought of him and his tales of woe brought a smile to her face. No wonder Maddy had told him he couldn't complain, because he definitely didn't mince words or hold back on speaking his thoughts aloud.

After the hockey game they'd watched together two nights ago—which the Falcons had won by two—Lindsey hadn't seen Nelson except for once in passing. He'd asked her if she needed any more help moving boxes. *No.* And she'd asked him how his knee was doing. *Fine.*

They'd both continued on their way, in opposite directions going down the hallway, but Lindsey was pretty sure he'd turned to look at her before she went outside. Nelson was a unique guy, and he was kind of a nice distraction from all the pressure of starting completely over in a new location. Not to mention dealing with the filing of her report to her former law firm. Dawson still wanted her to press charges, but with every hour that passed in Pine Valley, the more distant all the stuff about Paul became.

Lindsey stepped from her room and headed out of the bed and breakfast. She couldn't stay here much longer, because the price would eat up her savings quickly, so later this afternoon, she'd be meeting with a realtor to look at condos and apartments to rent. Dawson told her having realtor Jeff Finch show her around would be a lot faster than looking up rentals online and calling each place to schedule a visit.

She pulled up her playlist on her phone, then put in her Bluetooth ear buds. The morning was cool and windy, but she was determined to go running. Dawson had told her about a couple of route choices, and she took the shorter one so that she could break herself in. The sunrise changed the sky to pale gold and crystal blue as she set off. The first mile was torture. Various muscles hurt at different times. By the second mile, she decided that she would live and that running wasn't so bad after all. That changed halfway through the third mile. The aches returned, and so did a sharpness in her side.

Finally, half a mile from the bed and breakfast, she slowed to walk. Perhaps she'd started out too fast and had expected too much. Her phone rang, surprising her because of the early hour. It was barely seven in the morning. When she looked at the incoming number, she nearly stopped breathing.

Paul.

What was he doing calling her? And then she knew. Of course. She sent the call to voicemail prematurely. And ... sure enough, a moment later, the voicemail icon popped up with his message. Her heart stuttered. And her stomach felt like she'd swallowed a rock. She thought about waiting until she was with Dawson to listen to it, but the rock in her stomach grew heavier and heavier.

She was almost to the bed and breakfast, and although her body was cooling down and she was feeling quite chilly, she continued around the building and headed toward the gazebo behind the building. The wind rattled through the budding trees, and the fragrance of blossoms should have been comforting, but her stomach only twisted harder.

She sat on the cold wooden bench and listened to the voicemail.

"What the hell, Lin? I read the report you filed, and you know it's complete lies. I don't know what idiot lawyer would represent you, but you'd better bet that I'm going to be filing a lawsuit against you. For sexual harassment. Yep, you heard me. How does it feel to have the tables turned? Wenches like you think you can get away with teasing men, then dumping them when you've gotten your promotions or raises or whatever twisted satisfaction you're looking for. No more. It stops with me."

Paul proceeded to call her a few choice words, then hung up after more threats. Lindsey saved the message and lowered the phone. Her hands were trembling, and she couldn't catch a full breath. She knew Paul was a corrupt person, but his soul was truly ugly. And she didn't think for one moment that his threats were idle. She wished she could call Dawson right now, but she knew it was a court day for him.

Lindsey leaned forward and rested her elbow on her knees, keeping her phone gripped between her hands. She stared at the ground and the few leaves that were strewn there. The morning had started out with such hope and newness, but now she felt like she'd been dragged backward a hundred steps.

"Lindsey?" a voice said from the direction of the bed and breakfast.

Oh no. Tyler Nelson. What was he doing out here so early? Another hike?

She didn't lift her head, didn't move. Maybe he'd get the hint and leave her alone.

"You're freezing," he said, his voice closer now. "Do you want my jacket?"

She shook her head, still not looking at him. But he set a jacket over her shoulders anyway. Then he sat next to her.

"What's wrong? Are you sick?"

"No," she said, her voice sounding hoarse. She lifted her head and exhaled. "Just got some bad news."

Their gazes connected, and she hated that his gray eyes were intent on her, not missing a thing. She didn't want to spill her miserable story to someone she'd barely met.

"You might need a new phone," he said. "You're about ready to crush that one."

Lindsey looked down at her hands. Her knuckles were white from gripping her phone so hard.

"Here," he said, placing his hand on hers, then he gently pried the phone from her hands. "You might need it later." He set the phone on the bench.

She said nothing.

He said nothing.

His jacket helped with the shivering, but only just.

After another minute, Nelson pulled out his phone and sent a text.

"You don't need to stay," she said, making a move to take off the jacket.

"Keep it on," Nelson said. "I told Maddy that I'm delaying our hike. No big deal. Do you want me to bring you a hot drink?"

Lindsey's eyes stung at his kindness. She wasn't going to let herself cry, though. He wasn't trying to make her go inside or asking her to tell him anything. He was just trying to make her comfortable.

"Something hot would be great," she said at last.

"I'll be back in a minute."

And he left.

Lindsey closed her eyes. She was going to be in for a pretty big fight against Paul. If he followed through with his threats, the case would hit the media. Maybe she should drop the case, but even as she considered it, she knew she couldn't. She pulled Nelson's jacket closer, encasing her hands. Her phone was still on the bench, and some emails chimed through, but she didn't look at them.

When Nelson returned, she felt more calm. He handed over a steaming mug of tea, and she took a careful sip. The wild-orange flavor was sweet, yet somehow strong and soothing.

Nelson sat by her again. She noticed for the first time what he was wearing. Those hiking boots and ratty jeans, along with a long-sleeved T-shirt. Dark gray, like his eyes. He smelled like soap and spice. Did he shower first thing in the morning or something?

"You know when we first met at the café?" she asked.

"When I nearly punched Dawson Harris?"

"Yeah, I didn't want to bring up that part, but I wanted to explain why I was there in the first place." She glanced at him, then away. "Why I'm in Pine Valley at all."

She'd told him a little about her former firm the other night when they were watching the hockey game, but not the real reason why she'd left everything to come to Pine Valley.

"There's more than what you told me?" he asked, his gray eyes steady on hers.

Somehow she trusted those gray eyes, although she couldn't exactly explain why. Yeah, she'd googled the heck out of his name and she hadn't found any reported felonies or petty crimes. Not that she expected to, but assumptions had sometimes gotten her into bad situations. Like with Perkins and Gunner.

So she told Nelson about her former law firm. About the money she'd brought into the firm in just a few months, and how Mr. Gunner had told her she was on track to make partnership. It was a little harder to talk about Paul Locker and how he'd treated her. She left out the specific details, but judging by the storm in Nelson's gaze, she knew that he was reading between the lines.

Remarkably, he listened and didn't pepper her with questions as she spoke. Until the end. "The message on your phone was from this Paul Locker guy?" he asked, his eyes steely.

"Yeah."

"Can I listen to it?"

Lindsey hesitated. Sure, she'd have Dawson listen—he was representing her, after all. But Nelson was . . . a wild card.

All for You

"Um, I think it's going to be evidence," she said at last, "so I probably shouldn't be sharing it with those who aren't connected to the case."

Nelson's jaw flexed. "I don't know about all the legal stuff you just said, but maybe I can offer a different perspective." He picked up the phone while holding her gaze. "You know, an outsider's opinion."

She exhaled. Was he right? Or was she taking comfort in the fact that her burdens felt slightly less when talking to this man? As gut-wrenching as this entire situation with Paul was, she was feeling much better than she had felt when she'd first seen his name on her caller ID.

"Okay." She took the phone from Nelson so she could unlock it and pull up the voicemail.

She handed the phone back to Nelson, then she stood and paced while he listened to the message. She couldn't look at him, didn't want to see the expression on his face, because it would make her feel sick all over again.

A moment later, he set the phone down on the bench. He didn't move for a while, and she continued to pace, her stomach in knots. What did Nelson think? He'd heard almost everything now. So there was no secret that her life was a mess, and the train wreck was far from over. Maybe he'd ask for his jacket back and tell her good luck and that it was nice knowing her.

Lindsey stopped at the opposite end of the gazebo. The sun was well on its way across the horizon now, and the morning was beginning to warm bit by bit.

She heard the shuffle of steps and realized that Nelson had risen from the bench. He walked toward her, but she didn't turn around.

"Lindsey," he said, placing his hand on her shoulder. "I'm really sorry about what you're dealing with. Paul's a bastard."

She nodded, both agreeing with his pronouncement and feeling like crying at the same time.

"Although I know very little about the legal world, any judge will see right through him," Nelson continued.

"I hope so." The trembling in her voice had returned.

Nelson's hand moved from her shoulder to her upper back, and she turned toward him. Without a word, he pulled her against him, and she wrapped her arms around his sturdy waist. Everything about him was solid and warm, and as he moved his hand slowly along her back, she closed her eyes. Breathed him in. For a moment, Paul's accusations felt far away. In another life.

She wished it would stay that way, that she wouldn't have to return to reality.

Meanwhile, Nelson smelled really good, all male and clean and spicy, and the strength of his arms around her was like a barrier against all things Paul. But it wasn't like she could stay this way forever.

"Lindsey . . ." His voice was low, his touch intoxicating and calming at the same time.

She really needed to release him. Get in the shower. Organize her office. Find some clients. She exhaled, then drew away. Nelson dropped his hands, and Lindsey only wanted to step into his embrace again.

"Thank you," she said, smoothing her hair back, her hands trembling for a different reason now. "I really needed that hug."

He smiled, but his gaze was somber. "Any time."

She drew in another breath, then stepped away, reducing the temptation to do the opposite. She crossed the gazebo and picked up her phone. "Oh, your jacket." Slipping if off, she handed it to him.

He took the jacket but said nothing, only watched her with those dark gray eyes.

Lindsey took another step away, then another. "Have a good hike, and I'll see you . . . sometime." She turned then, hurrying to the building. She heard Nelson say goodbye, but she didn't slow.

She really needed some space and a moment to herself. A lot of moments.

Eight

Apparently the big-shot lawyer Dawson Harris drove a pristine red truck. Nelson's temper went down one point. At least the guy wasn't in a $200,000 sports car. Maybe he had some decency in him after all. It hadn't been hard to find information on Dawson, and Nelson had called the number listed on the website.

His call had gone to voicemail, as expected, but Nelson had been sure to leave a message that would ensure him a same-day reply. And yep. Less than an hour later, Dawson had called. And now they were meeting just after 7:00 p.m. in Dawson's office. The lights on the side of the building where Lindsey's office was were off, so hopefully that meant that she was gone for the day. A good thing in Nelson's mind, because he didn't know how well this conversation would go.

As Dawson parked his truck, Nelson opened the door of Maddy's Subaru and climbed out. Then he waited by the steps for Dawson.

"How are you doing?" Dawson said, his tone friendly.

The guy was wearing another expensive suit, which didn't surprise Nelson. "*I'm* fine," he said. "Thanks for meeting me."

"No problem." Dawson led the way up the steps to the building. He unlocked the front door, then flipped on lights as the two of them entered the building. They bypassed Lindsey's office, where the door was shut, and Dawson opened the door to the second office.

There, Nelson took a seat in the leather chair across the huge desk from Dawson.

"I listened to Paul Locker's message on Lindsey's phone," Nelson began, not wanting to waste a moment. Since seeing Lindsey this morning, he hadn't been able to think of anything else.

Dawson nodded. "She told me. And the voice recording will be submitted as evidence if the case gets before a judge." He shuffled a few papers, then focused his brown eyes on Nelson. "Before we get into all of this, I need to know what your intentions are toward Lindsey. You only met her a few days ago, so needless to say, I'm surprised at your insistence to meet with me."

"Fair enough," Nelson said. "We're staying at the same place and have talked a few times. I guess you could say we've become friends. But when she told me about her previous firm this morning, I didn't want her to be alone in this fight. Yeah, she has you as a lawyer, but . . . I guess I want to help."

Dawson didn't blink, didn't respond. Then he said, "I've done my own checking up on you. So far, things look clean, and I hope that's the case."

Nelson held Dawson's gaze. "You don't have to worry about me. What I want to know is how someone like Paul Locker can get away with being such a creep? In my world, this would have been taken care of within a few hours with a visit and a few choice words."

Dawson lifted a hand. "First of all, Paul isn't going to get away with anything. And second, the legal process takes time and endurance. Months at the very least, possibly longer if Paul follows through on his threat."

Nelson clenched his jaw. Dawson's answers were all textbook, telling Nelson what he wanted to hear. "And you think you can go up against a major, established law firm? You have what? One or two paralegals working for you?"

"One," Dawson said, his tone less friendly now. "I'm not worried about my ability to defend Lindsey. Her case is solid, as you know, and in the end, she'll come out on top. Which will be well deserved."

Nelson couldn't argue with the fact that Lindsey deserved to win the case. The whole situation was frustrating to him, whether or not he was coming to like Lindsey more than he should. All of that aside, he'd watched his sister work hard for her degree and put in overtime hours at her job. Becoming successful in her own right. And he knew there was no way he'd sit around while lawyers emailed motions back and forth if this had happened to his sister.

For a panicked moment, he wondered if she'd ever dealt with a "Paul" in her life. It made him feel cold all over to think of it, even more so if she hadn't told him. She'd be getting a surprise call from him later tonight.

"So what are the next steps?" Nelson asked, knowing that his tone sounded hard and possibly skeptical.

Dawson leaned back in his chair. "We filed Lindsey's report to the firm yesterday, and we're waiting for an official response from the firm."

"So what was Paul's phone call about?"

"Separate from the firm, he could countersue for personal damages," Dawson said in a smooth tone. "Which of course would affect the litigation of the current case. Make things more complicated. But the end result will be the same."

Nelson nodded. He felt better, but not much better.

"Look, Tyler—"

"Nelson," he corrected.

"Nelson," Dawson amended. Leaning forward, he steepled his hands on the desk. "Lindsey and I go way back to law school. We've been friends for a long time. I'm not going to let anything happen to her. And if . . . as you say . . . this case turns out to be more than I can handle, I'll bring in joint counsel."

This was what Nelson was looking for. To know that Lindsey wasn't going to be at a single person's mercy. "Okay."

"Anything else?" Dawson asked.

"One more thing." Nelson leaned forward as well. "What would happen if I did make a visit? Had a chat with Paul?"

Dawson stilled, his brown eyes gazing right into Nelson's soul. This was man to man now. No lawyers or hockey players involved. Something flashed in Dawson's eyes. "I told Lindsey to change her cell number, so hopefully Paul won't be calling her again. But let's just say that if you do make a visit, I don't want to know any details. I can't be discredited as her lawyer in any way. Understand?"

Nelson felt like grinning. "I understand."

The continuing conversation after that was much less tense, and Dawson explained how the process worked and all the hoops that had to be jumped through. By the time Nelson left the lawyer's office, he was grateful for a career that was more cut and dried. Sure, sometimes the refs screwed up or he had to put up with dysfunctional teammates and a cold-hearted coach, but the rules of the game made hockey straightforward and not dependent on the decision of a single judge.

When Nelson climbed into Maddy's Subaru, he decided

to make a detour to the Main Street Café. He'd been suffering through Maddy's concoctions of green smoothies and hard-as-a-rock granola for long enough. Ending a long day with something with meat in it would be more than welcome.

The café looked warm and welcoming as Nelson parked in front of the place. He could practically smell the warm food before he even climbed out of the car. He strode to the door, and his hand paused on the door handle. Through the glass windows, he saw Lindsey sitting with a man. It was like déjà vu. Although this man wasn't Dawson Harris.

The guy was dark-haired and wore khakis and a leather jacket over a sweater. A bit preppy, in Nelson's opinion.

Nelson exhaled and opened the door. He wasn't going to make a big deal out of anything. Besides, Lindsey looked like she was having a perfectly good time with this other guy. So what if Nelson had shared an amazing hug with her that morning? It wasn't like they were dating or anything close to that. The guy across from Lindsey had a laptop open and was pointing to something on the screen. Maybe he was *another* lawyer? How many lawyers could there be in the small town of Pine Valley?

Nelson headed to the counter to order dinner. He wasn't going to interrupt the two at the table. This time he'd let Lindsey take the lead. Truth was, in a couple of weeks, if all went as planned, he'd be back in Vegas fighting for his position. And Lindsey would stay in Pine Valley, building her business.

A teenager was at the counter, and his silver braces caught the light as he smiled. "What can I get you, sir?"

"How's the chicken pot pie?" Nelson asked.

"My favorite thing here."

"I'll have two then," Nelson said. "And a couple of those brownies. Plus a water bottle."

"Sure, thing," the teen said and rang up the price.

After paying and picking up the water bottle, Nelson turned to see Lindsey looking over at him. Well, he couldn't be so nonchalant now.

"Hey," she said with a smile.

He liked that smile. Very much. It meant she was feeling better compared to this morning.

"Hey." He walked toward the table.

The guy she was with stood from his chair. "You're Tyler Nelson," he said. "When Lindsey told me you were in town, I wasn't sure I believed her."

The guy's blue eyes were filled with admiration.

So maybe this wouldn't be so bad. "Yeah, do you follow hockey?"

The guy chuckled. "Sure do." He stuck out his hand. "I'm Jeff Finch. Nice to meet you."

Nelson shook the guy's hand briefly.

"Sit with us," Lindsey said.

It wasn't an invitation that Nelson could turn down, although he wasn't liking the way that Jeff Finch turned and grinned at Lindsey. How did they know each other? Was he from her old firm, or maybe she was dating him . . . ?

Then Nelson saw the laptop screen, which displayed a condo complex. "Looking for a place to live?"

"Yeah," Lindsey said. "Jeff's helping me. He's a realtor."

Nelson looked at Jeff with new eyes, much kinder eyes. "Great." Nelson shifted his gaze to the screen. "Looks like a nice place."

"It has tons of amenities," Jeff said. "I was just telling Lindsey here that this complex is the newest one in Pine Valley." He clicked on something and pulled up a map. "Phase one is built and ninety percent leased or sold. Phase two is currently under construction. There's a pool, two hot tubs, a park for kids . . ."

As Jeff Finch droned on about the amenities that they could read for themselves on the website, Nelson looked over at Lindsey. She'd been watching him, and now her gaze shifted away. Then back again.

Had she been checking him out? Whatever she'd been doing, she wasn't shying away from looking at him now. Something had changed between them, and Nelson wasn't sure what. But she was looking at him differently . . . like she was really seeing him . . . and she was *interested.* Which of course was ridiculous. Whatever friendship had budded between them was going to be pretty short-lived. At least in person. Nelson was hoping to keep in touch with her by phone once he returned to Vegas, if for nothing else than to follow up on the case with Paul Locker.

"How are you?" Nelson asked Lindsey in a quiet voice, despite the fact Jeff Finch was still expounding about the wonders of central heating and the weight room at the club house.

"Fine," she whispered. "How's your knee?"

"Better than yesterday," he said.

She smiled, and he was pretty sure his heart skipped a beat. Her blue eyes were the color of the Vegas sky in summer. And her minimal makeup had exposed her dash of freckles. He wanted to lean in, breathe in the perfume that he could smell.

"Your dinner, sir," a voice said above him. The teen had arrived with a couple of plates, a fork, and napkins. One plate held the chicken pot pies, the other brownies.

"Anyone want a brownie?" Nelson asked.

"I already ate," Jeff said.

But Lindsey's eyes had locked onto the brownies.

Nelson slid the plate closer to her. "Help yourself."

"You're probably starving," Lindsey said, pushing the plate back. "I can't take your food."

Nelson slid the plate toward her again. "Maddy is going to kill me if she finds out that not only did I have dinner here, but I also ate brownies. So really, if you eat one, you might not only be doing me a favor, but saving my life."

Lindsey laughed.

"Who's Maddy?" Jeff asked.

"The physical therapist from hell," he said. "Uh, *heck*."

Lindsey smirked.

"I mean, the best physical therapist in the country," Nelson continued, "and her whole focus is on returning me to my former glory."

Jeff chuckled. "Sounds like there's an interesting story there." He clicked on the laptop again and said, "Now, if you want to wait for phase two, then you'll have the option of . . ."

Nelson tuned out Jeff and took a bite of the chicken pot pie. The flaky, buttery crust and steaming goodness was ambrosia to his stomach. And sitting by Lindsey was an unexpected perk. If only Jeff would take himself elsewhere, this night wouldn't be half bad.

"I'll take one of those condos, Jeff," Lindsey said. "Whatever is available. I want to move in as soon as possible."

Nine

It had been a long day, filled with the ups and downs of getting her number changed and then looking at places with Jeff Finch. Maybe Lindsey was jumping in too fast when she told Jeff to draw up the paperwork for the condo as soon as possible. But the place was in her price range, and she didn't want to spend another day, or three, looking at other places. If Pine Valley worked out, she'd have plenty of time later to look around for a place to buy. For now, a one-year lease wasn't something to lose sleep over.

When Jeff had gathered his things to leave the café, he offered to drop Lindsey at the bed and breakfast, but Nelson had interrupted and said he had a car and was going the same direction. So here Lindsey sat, in Maddy's Subaru, while Nelson navigated the small-town streets. Sitting in a car with Nelson put them in close proximity with each other, not to mention that it isolated them from other people or distractions. It was just her . . . and Nelson.

His hair was combed more than usual tonight, and he was clean-shaven. She wondered why he seemed more dressed up than usual. He wore dark jeans, a button-down shirt, and loafer shoes that matched his belt. She hadn't pictured Nelson as a belt-wearing type of guy. Not when she'd only seen him in ratty jeans or athletic shorts. Oh, and the hockey uniform she'd spied during her google searches. But the belt was a nice touch, and if Lindsey was going to be completely honest, sexy on him.

So not where she wanted her thoughts to go. Nelson lived in Vegas and would be leaving in, what? A couple of weeks? Three at the most? Then what? He'd become an interesting and fond memory. She might watch a little more hockey, catch a few of his games, think of him as a guy whom she'd once blurted all her problems to . . .

"Wanna take a detour?" Nelson asked, cutting into her increasingly misdirected thoughts.

They were nearly to the bed and breakfast.

But she wasn't much looking forward to saying goodbye to Nelson and holing up in her room with a stack of contacts to begin emailing. Courtesy of Dawson. So she said, "What did you have in mind?"

"When we were hiking down the mountain this morning, we passed by another hiker—Dr. McKinney or something," Nelson said. "He said that just past the area we were hiking is a small herd of elk. They're nesting this time of year. Coming down from the higher elevations. We could go see them."

"Don't tell me you're turning into a nature boy after all."

Nelson laughed.

Lindsey sighed a happy sigh. She loved his laugh.

"Is that a yes?" he asked.

"I'm up for watching some elk in the dark."

Nelson slowed the car and did a U-turn. "The moon's out."

And yes, it was. The full moon was bright, and as they drove up the canyon road past the Pine Valley Lodge, Lindsey watched the moon winking through the pine trees. This place really was gorgeous. Dawson had told her that the summers were the best. Perfect temperature. Wildflowers all over the mountain. Crystal-blue streams.

Not that Lindsey would be hanging out in nature much.

"I think this is it," Nelson said, pulling onto a dirt road. The Subaru bumped along for a few minutes. Then the road opened into a wide meadow. A fence separated the road from the meadow.

At first, Lindsey didn't see anything, but when Nelson turned off the headlights of the car, her eyes adjusted. Dark forms were scattered throughout the meadow. Some standing, some lying down.

"Wow, there really are elk," she said, leaning forward in the car to peer through the windshield.

"Let's go out." Nelson looked over at her. "Are you going to be okay in those high heels?"

She looked down at her shoes. "I think so."

He nodded. "My jacket's in the back seat."

"I can't keep taking your clothes."

Nelson reached between the front seats to grab the jacket in the back, and his arm brushed hers.

Lindsey leaned away to give him more room and to command her pulse to slow down.

"Here." Nelson handed her the same jacket she'd worn that morning. Full circle.

"Are you sure?" she asked.

"I'm sure." He opened his door, effectively cutting off their conversation.

She pulled on the jacket, and a few seconds later, Nelson had reached her side of the car. He opened the door and held out his hand.

Why was she so nervous all of a sudden? She put her hand in his, and he helped her stand, but then . . . he didn't let go of her hand as they walked to the fence. Maybe he was worried about her tripping in her shoes over the uneven ground? Lindsey tried to decide how she felt about Nelson's large, warm hand enclosed around hers.

She could admit that it felt nice. More than nice.

They stopped at the fence, and Nelson kept a hold of her hand as they stood close together. She tried to focus on the elk, picking out different sizes of them and wondering about their quiet lives out here. But in truth, she was thinking about Nelson's fingers and his palm and how his arm was nestled against her and how much she liked his scent.

"What a life for an elk," she said. "Full of peace."

"Except for hunting season," Nelson said, squeezing her hand.

She smiled. "Except for that." Her gaze moved upward to the dark sky and glittering stars. "The sky seems so much larger out here."

Nelson looked up too. "I think that's a shooting star," he said, pointing.

She caught the streak of light. "Are you sure?"

"Make a wish."

So she did.

They were silent for a moment. "Did you make a wish?" she asked him, casting him a sideways glance.

"I did," he said.

She turned to face him, keeping a hold of his hand but linking their fingers. "What was it?"

He chuckled. "I can't tell you."

"Why not?"

"Then it won't come true." He looked down at her, and even in the light of the moon and stars, she felt the intensity of his gaze.

He was so close, and although only their hands were touching, she felt warm all over despite the chill of the night.

"Do you have a girlfriend, Nelson?"

One of his brows arched. "I wouldn't be out here holding your hand if I did." His thumb slowly brushed across her hand, back and forth, back and forth.

Goose pimples raced along her arms at the slow caress. "What are you all dressed up for?" she asked in a quiet voice.

Nelson seemed to hesitate, then he said, "I met with Dawson earlier."

She couldn't have been more surprised. "Why?"

He didn't answer for a few seconds.

"Nelson?" she prompted.

"I, uh . . ." He released her hand and leaned against the fence. "I wanted to ask him some questions about what he's doing to stop Paul Locker."

Lindsey stared at Nelson, although he wasn't looking at her. He was gazing at the elk, apparently fascinated by them now. She didn't know what to say. Or to think. Finally, she said, "Dawson's a good lawyer."

"Oh, believe me, he assured me of that," he said. "That guy doesn't lack confidence." Nelson turned to face her then and reached for her hand again. He drew her close and set his hands on her hips.

Oh boy. Her heart betrayed her, thumping like mad, while her body wanted to lean into him even more.

Then she understood. Clearly. She placed her hands on his forearms. His skin was warm, and she could feel the outline of his muscles. "Don't even think about it, Tyler Nelson."

His brows lifted a touch. "Think about what?"

"Whatever it is you're thinking of doing," she said. "Don't go find Paul. Stay away from him. You can't get caught up in this, because it could get ugly in the press. And you need to keep your pristine record."

"Dawson said it could take months or even longer," he said. "That's bullsh—"

"I know," she cut in. "That's how it works."

"In the meantime, the guy lives his life," Nelson said in a slow voice, "with nothing stopping him from treating a woman the same way again. I don't like it."

Lindsey almost smiled at Nelson's protectiveness, but there was nothing humorous about Paul. "I don't like it either. But please don't do anything. The system will take care of it."

Nelson didn't look too convinced.

Lindsey moved her hands up his arms, until they were resting on his shoulders. The solid curve of his shoulder rippled beneath her hands, and it also brought her much closer to him. She tilted her head. "Nelson, please don't do anything."

The edge of his mouth lifted. "Are you trying to sweet-talk me?"

"Is it working?" she asked.

His gaze dropped to her mouth. "Yes."

"Good." She moved her hands behind his neck, her fingers sliding through his hair. "Promise me you won't have any contact with Paul."

Nelson slid his hands behind her waist and up her back, pulling her closer. Their faces were only inches away now.

"Promise?" she whispered.

He leaned down, and she closed her eyes.

The first touch of his lips on hers was gentle. Questioning.

He drew back for a second, and she kept her eyes closed, her face upturned. Waiting.

"I promise," he whispered back.

She started to smile, but then he kissed her again, stopping that smile. His second kiss wasn't as tentative, and she melted into his warmth and want. She grasped the edges of his collar, and he buried one hand in her hair as he kissed her more deeply, more intently. Taking and giving.

She couldn't feel her feet, and she wondered if she was floating. The solid warmth of Nelson's body surrounding hers made her feel safe, secure. Her thoughts raced, her skin buzzed, her heart thrummed. So. She was kissing Tyler Nelson. A pro hockey player who would be returning to Vegas in a couple of weeks. Was this some sort of desperate reaction to all the stress she'd been under?

Or had Nelson come into her life at the precise moment that she needed him?

Because she was really feeling that need like a deep ache.

Nelson was the one who had to break off the kiss, since Lindsey was quickly losing all reasoning. He drew away, and leaned his forehead against hers, both of them catching their breath.

"Wow," he whispered.

That about summed it up. "Yeah, wow."

He pulled her tightly against him, and she buried her face against his neck. Breathing him in as the tingles started all over again. But she didn't move, didn't try to kiss him again. For this moment, being held by Nelson, with the cool air like a soft caress, would be something she never wanted to forget.

Ten

Nelson raked a hand through his hair, then answered the Facetime call from Coach. Nelson already knew that Coach talked to Maddy every few days for updates, but this was the first time Nelson had talked to him. A 6:30 a.m. call didn't bode too well.

"Maddy called me with some concerns," Coach said the second the connection was made.

Coach Graydon was a no-nonsense type of guy and ran his team like a tight ship. He also didn't communicate much beyond the sport. He was one of the highest-rated coaches in the league, but it could be said that the man had no life outside the sport or interest in his players' personal lives in the least. And now, Coach's dark brows pulled together in apprehension didn't make Nelson relax.

"What concerns?" Nelson asked, although he already knew. Maddy hadn't been quiet about the time Nelson had spent with Lindsey. She'd moved yesterday into her new place, and Nelson had helped her get things set up, including assembling a couple of bookcases. He'd hoped to steal another kiss, but that hadn't happened yet.

Things with Lindsey were definitely tentative. They lived a state apart. She was starting over. He was trying to salvage his career. Maddy had complained that a romantic distraction was the last thing Nelson needed. And Nelson would have completely agreed with that type of logic if the woman had been anyone other than Lindsey.

Lindsey was ... unexpected. She was intelligent and witty, and she didn't buy into any of his complaining. Nelson still hadn't decided which look he liked best on Lindsey. Her dressy, no-nonsense high heels, or the jeans and T-shirt she'd worn when he'd helped her move, or the leggings and tank shirt she wore when out running.

Last night, she'd laughed when he'd told her he wanted to count her freckles. She'd dodged him, but then he'd caught her in a bear hug. Holding her had made him forget his original statement.

"Nelson," his coach said in his grumbling voice. "Pay attention."

Nelson blinked. *Uh, right.* "I'm listening, Coach."

The line between Coach's brows only deepened. "Maddy says you're dating a woman in Pine Valley and eating carbs."

Well ... getting right to the point. "I've helped Lindsey move into her apartment, and we've spent some time together. But we're not *dating*, sir. I'm well aware of my reasons for being here, and I haven't missed one workout session with Maddy."

Coach stared through the phone, straight into Nelson's eyes.

"I'm also overloaded on the whole foods and greens," he said. "We both know I can handle a few carbs."

"Not if it slows down the healing process," Coach said. "I don't need to tell you what happened with Ben last game."

"I saw," Nelson said. The Falcons had won by one point again, after Ben let two goals through. The game was too close of a call for anyone to be pleased or in a celebratory mood.

"We need you focused," Coach continued. "You have an MRI scheduled for this afternoon. I want the results immediately."

"Sure thing, Coach," Nelson said, when in fact his stomach had twisted. Yeah, an MRI would be good, but he was already feeling claustrophobic thinking about it. Ironic, he knew. His hockey goaltender uniform should make him claustrophobic. But it was nothing compared to the narrow tube he had to stay absolutely still inside of, even if it was only the lower half of his body.

When Nelson hung up with Coach, he scrubbed a hand through his hair and stared out the window. Dawn was well on its way, and the sky forecasted a clear and cold day in Pine Valley. He missed that Lindsey wasn't staying in the bed and breakfast anymore. But at least he did have her cell number now. Maybe he'd ask her to come with him to the MRI for, well, moral support.

No.

She was probably busy, working on that client list of hers.

Nelson picked up his phone again and sent a text. *Are you extremely busy this afternoon, as in lockdown, saving-the-world meetings?*

She was probably out running or unpacking or still sleeping. He didn't expect her to call him right away, but that's what she did. Nelson's pulse skittered when he saw who was calling. Maybe Coach was right and Nelson was getting distracted.

But that didn't stop the smile that bloomed on his face as he answered. "Did I wake you?"

"What would you do if I told you yes?"

He could hear the smile in her voice, and that made him inordinately pleased. He crossed to his bed and settled against the stacked-up pillows. "I would apologize first, then ask if you wanted to go to breakfast."

"Maddy's setting you free?"

"Uh, no."

Lindsey laughed. "That's what I thought. I don't want you to get in trouble with your boss."

"Physical therapist," Nelson corrected. "But yeah, I can see where you'd think she was my boss. But speaking of bosses. My coach just called."

"Oh?" she said.

Nelson heard the trepidation in her voice and didn't know what to make of it. "Yeah. I'm getting another MRI this afternoon. Coach wants to evaluate the improvement. Ben really struggled this last game."

"Yeah," Lindsey said. "I was with you."

They'd watched the game together, and although Nelson had tried to keep his yelling at the television at a minimum, he couldn't suppress it all.

"Sometimes I hate that I got injured," Nelson said. "Well, I hate it every shi—*shining* second. The MRI better reveal something good."

"I'm sure it will," Lindsey said. "So, about your very vague text . . . Do you want me to come with you?"

Nelson exhaled as relief and gratitude coursed through him. "Would you?" he asked in a quiet voice.

"Sure."

He sat up. "Really?"

She laughed. "Really. I'm my own boss, remember. Unlike some people I know."

"Ha ha," he deadpanned. But he was ecstatic. Who knew

he'd ever look forward to an MRI? "Can I pick you up from your office about 2:00?"

"I'll be there."

The smile in her voice made Nelson wish his MRI was this morning. Say, in about twenty minutes. "Are you sure you don't want to play hooky with me and get breakfast?"

"It's not that *I* don't want to, Mr. Goaltender," Lindsey said in a soft tone. "But I think you'd better listen to Maddy."

"Why are you always right?" Nelson teased. "Was that a requirement to get into law school?"

"Something like that," she said.

Nelson was reluctant to hang up, but he was supposed to meet Maddy three minutes ago, and he probably shouldn't be dragging out this conversation. When they hung up, Nelson stayed on his bed another minute.

He sent a text to his sister, who now knew something about Lindsey.

Hey, sis, talked to Coach. Who is not happy that I'm seeing Lindsey. Do you think I should say anything to her?

The three dots bounced before Becca's reply came back. *Haha. Love it that my bro is smitten. It's about time. But don't put Lindsey in the middle of your discussion with your coach, even though it's about her. Wait until you know where things are going with your recovery. Maybe you'll trip up the hospital steps and have to add another month.*

Nelson scoffed. *My first injury in twenty-nine years, and you think I'm now a klutz?*

Oh, I thought there was a reason you had to wear so many pads at your games, Becca texted.

You're full of jokes in the morning, aren't ya, sis?

Learned it from the best, bro, Becca wrote, adding a winking emoji.

Your days of giving me advice are numbered, Nelson texted.

Becca texted back several emojis including a laughing face, a heart-eyes face, and the 1-2-3 icon.

Nelson chuckled, then pushed off his bed. He was now almost ten minutes late meeting Maddy. Maybe Coach was right. Nelson needed to keep his focus, because at no time during the conversation with Lindsey had he regretted coming to Pine Valley. And he should regret it because it meant he was in therapy for an injury and missing key games before the playoffs. Yet ... if he hadn't been injured, he'd never have met Lindsey Gerber.

A knock on the door sent a jolt of adrenaline through him.

"Nelson, you in there?"

"Coming, Maddy." He grabbed his jacket. Then he headed out the door and saw Maddy down the hall.

She cast a glance over her shoulder, her gaze assessing.

Nelson no longer limped, but he wasn't walking as fast as he wanted to be. Hopefully the MRI would give everyone answers.

Maddy had already started the car by the time he climbed in the passenger side.

"Sorry, Coach called," he said. It was the truth, but not the entire truth.

"Yeah," Maddy said, pulling out of the parking lot. "He called me too. Told me about the MRI he scheduled. I can drive you there."

"About that." Nelson paused. "Can I drive myself?"

Maddy threw him a sharp glance. "Taking Lindsey?"

Might as well own up to it. "Yeah. My last MRI was a bit of a fiasco. I think having Lindsey there will help."

Maddy pursed her lips.

Nelson wasn't really in the mood to defend Lindsey again today; besides, as long as he was on the trajectory to full recovery as scheduled, could Coach or Maddy really complain? Nelson looked out the side window at the passing buildings of Main Street. When Maddy didn't turn up the road that led to the ski resort, he said, "Where are we going?"

"To the rec center," Maddy said. "We'll work in the weight room."

"All right." They were back to business.

Nevertheless, the hours dragged as he did the weight-lifting rotation, then swam several laps in the rec center pool. Finally, he went into a late-morning yoga class.

"Helloooo," the yoga instructor said, her lively gaze on Nelson. "I'm Leslie, and you are . . . ?"

"Tyler Nelson." He didn't like the way the woman was ogling him. Sure, it happened. Frequently. And he didn't always mind it.

"Welcome, Tyler Nelson," Leslie said with a broad smile.

He mumbled a thanks and headed to the very back row and took an empty mat.

More eyes followed him. The class was all women, with the exception of a very thin man.

Where had Maddy gone? Had she taken a break?

Nelson tried to think of good things, positive things, as Leslie led the class into a series of warm-up stretches. Which did feel nice, by the way. Nelson proceeded with caution, testing out the strength of his knee, but he felt nothing amiss.

After the hour of yoga, Nelson made a quick escape, avoiding more questions from Leslie. He found Maddy in the lobby, reading a book on her Kindle.

"How was the class?" she asked as he approached.

"You ditched me," Nelson said.

Maddy tucked her Kindle into her bag. "I'm not the one in physical therapy. How's the knee?"

"Decent," Nelson said. "But I'm done with that class."

Maddy raised her brows. "Oh?"

"Yeah, let's go," Nelson said. "I need to get a shower in before the MRI so I don't scare away the hospital staff."

Once back in his room, Nelson hit the shower, then dressed quickly. In truth, his knee was aching more today than it had in the past three days. It worried him a bit, so maybe the MRI had been a good call by Coach.

Nelson was running a few minutes late by the time he reached the law offices. Lindsey was perched on the edge of the porch step wearing a silky blue blouse, black slacks, and black high heels. Her dark hair fell about her shoulders.

He parked and climbed out as she rose and walked toward the car.

Seeing her and knowing that she was willing to come to the MRI with him made his pulse skip. He was grateful. Not only for her friendship but for who she was and how he felt when he was around her.

"Hey," Lindsey said, slowing her step.

Nelson kept walking until he reached her. "You look beautiful."

"Trying to butter me up?" she asked with a smile. "I already said I would come."

Nelson grasped her hand, and her fingers curled around his. He leaned down and kissed her cheek, even though he wanted to kiss her more than that. "You smell good."

She slapped a hand on his chest. "You say that a lot."

He only smiled and tugged her hand. They walked to the car, and he opened the door for her. After she slid into the seat, he shut the door.

When he slid into the driver's side, she touched his arm and asked, "How are you feeling?"

He loved how she so casually touched him. "Nervous," he said. "But I'm glad you're coming."

She squeezed his arm. "You'll do fine."

At the next stop sign, he grasped her hand and linked their fingers. "Thanks again for coming, Lindsey, I mean it."

She met his gaze, and her blue eyes held his. "You're welcome."

He felt her sincerity through his entire body.

Eleven

Lindsey had never seen a person go from a healthy tan to sheer paleness in a matter of seconds. Until Nelson.

He'd kept a tight hold on her hand when they walked to the desk where they'd been directed. Nelson checked in, explaining who he was.

"Will I have to wear one of those gowns?" he asked.

"No sir," the nurse said. "Your athletic shorts will give us plenty of access to your knee. You won't even have to go all the way into the tube." She looked down at the iPad she held. "It looks like you can't have a Valium?"

"My PT is pretty strict with my diet," he said.

The nurse gazed at Nelson for a moment. "Okay, then, follow me."

They followed the nurse to the MRI room.

Lindsey knew she couldn't go inside with Nelson, but he was still holding her hand. Okay, gripping her hand. It was kind of funny, yet it was also endearing. She felt like a mom with a small kid who didn't want to go to the doctor.

When they neared the MRI room, she said, "I can't go in there with you."

"Maybe they can make an exception," he said, his gaze sliding to hers. A sheen of perspiration had appeared on his forehead. "I don't think I can do this. Maybe I'll take that Valium after all."

"If you need it, take it."

Nelson exhaled. "No. I'll be fine."

He was looking rather pale.

"Come on, Mr. Goaltender." Lindsey wrapped her arm about his waist and steered him the last few steps toward the MRI room. "I've got you."

He draped an arm about her shoulder, and Lindsey would have felt a little cozy if they weren't in a hospital.

The nurse opened the door. "Ready?" she asked.

Nelson didn't even look at her. "Give me another minute."

The nurse nodded and disappeared inside.

Lindsey rubbed his back a little, finding his muscles tense. Then it was time. Even though they weren't alone, she wrapped her arms about his neck and drew close.

"I'll be right here the whole time," she said. "In that chair over there."

His gaze cut to the chair, then moved back to her face. She could feel the rapid beat of his heart. And she wondered if kissing him would help, but they were in the middle of a hospital. "You'll be fine," she murmured.

He nodded. His face was still pale, but the look in his eyes was more determined. Worried, but determined.

"Ready, Mr. Nelson?" a woman asked, cracking open the door. "I'm the MRI tech, and we'll make sure you're comfortable. What type of music do you like to listen to?"

That was all Lindsey heard before Nelson disappeared into the room. Well, he'd made it this far.

Personally, she thought that if he was really that stressed, he should have been able to take something for it. Lindsey took a seat and waited. She checked her phone for any new emails, but nothing was interesting enough to capture her attention.

The extra time gave her an opportunity to review her day, in which she'd set up several new client meetings with people to discuss their estate planning, living trusts, and wills. Dawson had been in the office part of the time and had given her updates on the case against Perkins & Gunner. There was no countersuit from the law firm, but that didn't mean that Paul Locker wouldn't bring one himself.

Dawson had already informed the firm that Lindsey had received a threatening voicemail from one of their partners. And now, Lindsey had to trust in the system of the law that she'd so valiantly studied and upheld.

She leaned her head against the wall. How long did an MRI take anyway? She was happy she could be here for Nelson, but every minute she spent with him only made her worry more about what was happening to her heart. She'd had a boyfriend in high school her entire senior year. Had dated in law school, but nothing serious. No one had time for serious in law school. And since getting hired at her first firm, she still hadn't had time for much else besides work.

But she was twenty-eight now, and Nelson was twenty-nine. Did people their ages have flings? Was this the norm for Nelson? What did he think? Of *her*? He was the one who'd be leaving soon, and although they hadn't really talked about what was going on between them, she couldn't imagine him having time to invest in any long-distance relationship. She'd googled that too. Not the "how to manage a long-term relationship" but the "average schedule for a professional hockey player."

During the off-season, he had plenty of commitments, not to mention required training and conditioning. As far as she knew there was no hockey rink in Pine Valley. Lindsey puffed out a breath. What was she thinking? That Tyler Nelson, one of the top goaltenders in the world, was going to move to Pine Valley?

The MRI door clicked open. Lindsey looked up as Nelson walked out.

The tech was talking to him, so Lindsey waited. When the tech went back into the room, Lindsey crossed to Nelson.

"How was it?" she asked.

He grasped her hand as his gray eyes connected with hers. "It's over."

She smiled. "Good job."

He tugged her closer, and she stepped forward into his arms. "Can we go get some carbs?" he asked, like he needed to get her permission.

Lindsey laughed. "Sure, where do you want to go? I'm assuming not the hospital cafeteria."

"You have time?"

She slid her hands over his shoulders and met his gaze. "I'm busy, but I don't exactly have twenty clients knocking on my office door."

"And a girl's gotta eat, right?" Nelson said, his gaze dropping to her lips.

"Right," she whispered.

"Okay, let's go."

She nodded but didn't step back, and he didn't release her. Her stomach decided to growl at that moment, and Nelson chuckled. "I should probably feed you. This was a lot of hard work."

Lindsey smirked and drew away.

They walked out of the hospital, and minutes later, they settled into Maddy's Subaru.

"Where we going?" Lindsey asked. "The café?"

"Nope," he said. "We're expanding our horizons. The owner of the bed and breakfast told me about a great barbeque place."

"Sounds good to me," Lindsey said. Was this a real ... date? It was more than casually hanging out. She'd gone to his medical appointment, and now he was taking her out to eat. Maybe she shouldn't analyze it so much.

But when Nelson took her hand as he drove to the restaurant, Lindsey knew that she was really going to miss him when he left Pine Valley.

The restaurant didn't look too busy when they pulled into the parking lot. It was probably because of the weird hour of three thirty. The sign on the restaurant read *Rick's BBQ*. Nelson opened his door, and Lindsey was about to pop hers open too when Nelson came around the front of the car. So this was a real date. Maybe?

He opened her door, and when she climbed out, he again linked their hands.

Neither of them said anything on the way to the restaurant. Nelson told the hostess they wanted a table for two, and they followed the hostess to where they were seated in a booth.

Lindsey sat a respectable distance from Nelson, but he had no such boundaries. He sat close enough to hold hands or drape an arm across her shoulders. Lindsey found herself wondering how Nelson felt about PDA.

"Here are your menus," the hostess said. "Your server will be here in a minute to take your drink orders."

"Great, thanks." Nelson opened his menu after the hostess left. "Can I order one of everything?"

Lindsey laughed. "I don't think anyone could eat that much, not even a hockey player."

Nelson fixed his gray eyes on hers, the edge of his mouth quirked. "Is that a challenge?"

"Don't you dare," she said. "I'm not going to be the one to explain to Maddy." She liked the humor in his eyes—so much better than the worry and panic over the MRI.

"I haven't eaten since this morning's protein shake, so I could do some serious damage right now."

"You're not supposed to skip meals," Lindsey teased.

Nelson shrugged. "I didn't want to puke at the hospital."

Oh. That.

"What can I get you to drink, folks?" a woman asked.

Lindsey looked up to see their server, a pretty blond woman who appeared to have rather large fake lashes and painted-on eyebrows. She was also smiling quite openly at Nelson. Maybe she was just the friendly sort and it came with her job description.

"Water for me," Nelson said.

"Me too, thanks," Lindsey added.

"Okaaay," the server said, keeping her gaze on Nelson. "Are you sure a big guy like you doesn't want something stronger?"

Nelson smiled. "I'm fine."

The server hesitated. "All righty then, I'll be back with your waters." She winked at Nelson, then practically sashayed away.

After she was out of earshot, Nelson scoffed. "Apparently she can call me a 'big guy,' but if I called a woman a 'big girl' . . ."

Lindsey smirked. "Yeah, double standard . . . except . . ."

Nelson arched a brow. "You're really going to go there?"

"You *are* kind of a big guy."

"Six four, two-forty," he said. "It's on my profile, but I'm probably two-thirty now with the abuse from Maddy. I mean, her loving concern. But I dare anyone to find an ounce of extra fat on me."

"Is that a challenge?"

"Come here, and you can check."

Lindsey laughed as he draped an arm about her and tugged her close.

"I believe you," she said. "You don't need to be so cocky about it. Not all of us can spend our lives being athletic."

He chuckled. "Believe me, that's not the first time I've heard that line."

She wanted to nestle against him, but they were in a public restaurant. So she took the arm around her and removed it, but kept a hold of his hand. "Well, I at least know one of your flaws," she teased.

"I have a lot more, but I'm good at hiding them."

"Hmm." Lindsey squeezed his hand. "As a lawyer, I'm pretty good at finding out the truth."

One side of his mouth lifted. "I'll look forward to that then." The gray of his eyes darkened into an intensity that spread warmth through her body until it reached to her toes.

She really wished they weren't in a restaurant right now, but it was probably a good thing.

When the server delivered the glasses of water, she was all smiles toward Nelson again. Lindsey took a long drink of water while he ordered three things on the menu. When it came Lindsey's turn to order, the server didn't fawn over her at all.

After the server left, Lindsey said, "I think you're her favorite."

Nelson smiled and shook his head. "I don't care about what our server thinks of me. What I want to know is, am I *your* favorite?"

His tone was teasing, but the words still made her

stomach flip. Yes, he was her favorite. But . . . "You're not so bad, Mr. Goaltender," she said in a light tone as she nudged his arm. "But the verdict is still out."

"Ouch," Nelson said. "I guess I still have some work to do. What are your plans tonight?"

Twelve

Nelson stared at the text on his phone. He and Lindsey had just left the restaurant and sat in the car. He'd invited her to a movie later in the evening, and she'd accepted. So much for cooling things off with her. He was feeling content, until the text from Coach came in.

The MRI results are in. Get to the hospital to review them, then conference me in.

"What is it?" Lindsey asked, probably because he'd been silent for an entire minute.

He told her about the text, then added, "I need to go to the hospital again."

"Do you want me to come?" she asked.

Nelson couldn't explain the relief that he felt. It wasn't an issue of facing an MRI tube again, but the results would be determining his immediate future. And he sort of wanted Lindsey as a part of that . . . He took her hand and pressed a kiss on it.

"Is that a yes?" she asked with laugh.

"Yeah." He wanted to do more than kiss her hand, but Coach was waiting.

He started the engine.

Walking into the hospital the second time that day hadn't been his plan.

They met with the doctor, and Nelson was able to conference in Coach so he could hear the prognosis.

"The healing is complete," the doctor said. "As you can see here, the sprain is no longer visible. Although that doesn't mean you shouldn't be cognizant of the injury. Your body is still in the active-healing zone."

Nelson nodded. He was both relieved and anxious. This meant . . .

"When can he return to full activity on the ice?" Coach cut in.

The doctor glanced at the calendar on the wall. "Friday he can start practicing. One more week until he's in a game."

Nelson should be shouting with joy, but he only felt a dull ache begin behind his eyes.

Coach asked more questions of the doctor, and Nelson barely heard the conversation. Lindsey had waited in the lobby because she said she didn't want to interfere with the privacy of the meeting, even though he'd told her he didn't mind. Now he'd have to tell her the news. Yeah, she knew he'd be heading back to Vegas soon. But not *this* soon.

After Nelson hung up with Coach, he thanked the doctor, then headed toward the waiting room.

He spotted Lindsey sitting on a chair, leafing through a magazine. Seeing her in that moment, before she saw him, made Nelson's heart hurt. He couldn't explain *why* exactly. It was like he was already missing her, even though they'd still have a couple of days together . . . if he chose. Surely Coach would want him heading home tomorrow. But Nelson planned to stay in Pine Valley until the last possible minute.

Before meeting Lindsey, he would have never imagined delaying practice or anything to do with hockey.

"How'd it go?" Lindsey looked up from the magazine to catch him staring at her. Her smile faded, which told him that he wasn't very good at hiding the news he was about to tell her.

She set down the magazine, then rose to her feet. "So you've been cleared to play?"

"Yeah." He scrubbed a hand through his hair as she approached. He wanted to go back in time to when they were at the restaurant, teasing each other. He didn't like the heaviness that had settled on his shoulders. "The doctor says I can return to practice on Friday, then start playing next week."

"Friday?" Lindsey echoed. "As in *this* Friday ... three days?"

He nodded, because his throat felt tight.

Lindsey's smile was bright when she said, "Well, that's great news. You're going to be playing again soon. Saving the season. Just what you wanted."

"Yeah," he said, although the word felt empty.

They continued through the hospital until they reached the parking lot. The cool spring air felt like a slap because the promise of warmth and budding trees producing fruit and leaves wasn't something that Nelson would be around to see. When had he become such a nature lover?

"Hey, I'm sure you have a lot to get ready for." Lindsey faced him as he opened the car door for her. "So don't worry about entertaining me."

He didn't know how to respond. Was she talking about the movie invitation or something more? He set his hand against the top of the car so that she wouldn't get inside yet. "I don't want to change our plans."

She exhaled, gazing at him with those clear blue eyes of hers. "Maybe it will be easier, Nelson. Think about it." She placed her hand on his arm. "You've been great, and I've helped you through a couple of things too. You're returning to Vegas in a couple of days, and I've got a business to establish here."

He looked down at the hand on his arm, then into her blue eyes again. "I don't think so."

Her brows shot up. "What?"

"I don't want to cancel our date tonight," he said, leaning close and lowering his voice. "And even though I have to get back to Vegas to finish out the season, I don't plan on cutting things off from you."

Lindsey bit her lip, and he saw the amusement in her eyes. Was she laughing at him? Had he been too over the top?

"So are we having the relationship talk?" she asked, a small smile escaping.

"Sure, why not?" he said. "I mean, I have a definitive departure date now, but I'm already thinking of retiring. Maybe tomorrow."

Lindsey's eyes widened. "You wouldn't dare!"

He chuckled. "No, I think I have a few good years left; besides, the pay is decent." He slipped an arm about her waist. She seemed to step easily into his arms, and he liked that very much. "So . . . I like you, Lindsey Gerber. Is that okay?"

She lifted her chin to meet his gaze. "I like you too, Tyler Nelson. But I don't see how—"

"Shh," he said, pressing a finger against her mouth. "Sometimes things fall into place without minute-by-minute planning. Let's just go with it . . . go with *us*."

She held his gaze, and it was a good feeling to see trust in her eyes. And affection. He could get used to that.

When she slipped her arms about his waist, he didn't

delay another second. He moved a hand behind her neck. Then he lowered his mouth to hers and kissed her in the hospital parking lot. She felt warm and soft, and she fit against his body with precision. He kissed her slowly, taking his time because he knew their time was limited.

She pressed closer, kissing him back, letting him know that she did care.

Where this would all lead, he didn't know, and he didn't want to waste time guessing. He wanted to stay in the moment, and in all the moments he had left with her. He moved his hand down her back, feeling her tremble as much as him. The more he was with her, the more he wanted to be with her.

"Lindsey," he whispered against her mouth, then he dipped his head to kiss her jaw.

She arched back a little, giving him more access to her neck. So he kissed her neck too. Her smell was sweet and intoxicating, and he wondered what he'd miss the most about her. Her blue eyes or her scent. Or maybe how she seemed to be aware of every little thing about him. Or how she kissed him back as if she dreamed of him at night as he dreamed of her.

He returned to kissing her mouth and soon became lost again.

Nelson didn't know how much time had passed when she drew away.

Placing a hand on his chest, she said, "Okay, I'll go to the movies with you."

"Charmed by my persuasive ways?" he asked.

Her very kissable lips lifted. "Something like that."

He kissed her again, but it was too brief, because she said, "Come on, big guy, we can't stay here all day."

"I think we can," he teased.

She pulled away from him and slipped past him into the passenger seat.

He groaned. "Fine." When he closed her door, he caught her smile. He hadn't told her that Coach thought dating in Pine Valley was a bad idea. But coaches didn't know everything, right? The man wasn't even married, so he wasn't necessarily an expert on relationships. Not that Nelson was thinking of getting married any time soon.

Now, that would be truly nuts.

He climbed into the Subaru and started the engine. "So, I'll drop you off wherever you want, and then I'll report to Maddy." He looked over at Lindsey. "She probably has some extreme conditioning she wants me to do. I'll text you with a time for a movie. You choose it."

When Lindsey's brows rose, he said, "What?"

"You don't have a movie in mind?" she said. "Like one of those action flicks?"

He pulled out of the parking lot. "I can't remember when I last saw a movie, so you can surprise me."

"Okay," Lindsey said. "This will be fun."

"Hopefully not to my detriment."

She took out her phone and pulled up the movie theater website. "Oh, found one. I've been wanting to see it."

"Which one?" he asked.

But she pressed the phone to her chest. "It will be a surprise."

Okay, he could live with that, because he'd be with her. And he didn't really care about the movie . . . it was just a way to keep her close.

She told him to take her back to the office, and when he watched her walk inside the building it felt like his heart was walking away with her.

Nelson drove back to the bed and breakfast. What was

happening to him? His emotions were all over the place. He'd kept things light with Lindsey, but in truth, he was hating the fact that he'd be leaving in two days.

He parked, then climbed out of his car. Once in his room, he texted his sister with the news since she'd told him to keep her posted. Then he texted Maddy that he was back from the MRI.

Maddy immediately replied to meet in the lobby in ten minutes. She wanted him doing an hour-long bike ride before it grew dark.

Nelson sighed. He was already wearing athletic shorts, so he changed into a T-shirt. Before he could leave his room, Coach called.

"Hi," Nelson said. "What's up?"

"What do you think about the news?" Coach asked. "I'll have Kris call you with the travel plans, but you'll be flying out tomorrow afternoon."

"That's Wednesday. I thought I'd leave Thursday night." Even a few more hours would be great.

"You want to be rested for Friday," Coach said. "Plus on Thursday, we've got a promo op with the team. We'll have a car pick you up at the airport."

It wasn't like Nelson could say no, and any arguing would only make Coach suspicious and ... lead to another argument.

After Nelson hung up with Coach, he strode out of his room. Tomorrow. He'd be leaving *tomorrow*. Unbelievable.

Maddy was waiting in front of the bed and breakfast with his bike.

"Heard the MRI results were positive," she said.

"Yeah," Nelson said, trying to keep the frustration out of his voice. "Thanks to your whipping me into shape. I fly out tomorrow."

Maddy didn't seem surprised. Maybe Coach had already informed her of the travel plans. "Good for you. I'll try to catch one of your games."

Nelson nodded, but he was done talking for now. He climbed onto his bike. He might have ridden a little faster than he normally did, because he was back to the bed and breakfast in forty-five minutes, drenched in sweat.

After locking up the bike next to where Maddy had kept hers, he headed to his room to shower. He was still grumpy, and he needed to snap out of it. He needed to stop thinking that after tomorrow he wouldn't see Lindsey for a while. Maybe months. Unless he could convince her to visit him in Vegas.

Thirteen

The movie critics had lied; either that or Lindsey's taste in movies was absolutely opposite of Rotten Tomatoes.

Nelson seemed to be absorbed in the movie, though. He'd happily finished off the tub of popcorn they were supposed to be sharing. Lindsey had maybe eaten three handfuls. And the soda. Well, Nelson had drawn the line there and gotten a water bottle, but Lindsey had chosen root beer, which she'd offered Nelson when he'd finished his water.

The hero in the movie had just stepped into another dimension, and Lindsey gave up trying to keep track of what was the past, present, or future. Nelson had told her he had to fly out tomorrow, so really, this was their last evening together. She marveled at how much she was dreading him leaving when they'd only been hanging out a short while. Could it even be considered dating?

Well, they had kissed, more than once, and she supposed that counted for something.

"Wanna ditch?" Nelson whispered in her ear.

"I thought you were enjoying the show," she whispered back.

"When the green man appeared, I think I lost interest," he said. "Either that or the little fairy thing with the giant teeth."

Lindsey stifled a laugh.

"Besides, the popcorn is gone," he continued, "and I really shouldn't have more, so leaving will help me in that department."

Lindsey turned her head to meet his gaze in the darkness of the theater. She couldn't see the color of his eyes, but she could certainly feel their intensity. And, boy, she had a hard time saying no to this man.

"Okay."

He was on his feet in an instant, his speed surprising her.

She joined him, and he grasped her hand as they left the theater.

When they stepped out into the cold, dark night, Lindsey said, "Now what, Mr. Goaltender? More elk watching?"

Nelson released her hand and draped his arm about her, pulling her close. Which felt nice, because the wind had picked up. "Whatever you want. Elk watching, a hospital tour of the MRI room, or . . . maybe we could visit the grocery store."

"The grocery store?" she asked. "Don't tell me you're thinking of food again after eating an entire tub of popcorn."

They stopped by the car that Nelson had once again borrowed from Maddy. "You ate some too."

She held her two fingers about an inch apart.

Nelson chuckled and opened her door.

She climbed in before he could kiss her in another parking lot. It was way too cold for that.

When he slid into the driver's seat, she said, "I'll choose the grocery store, but only because you have me curious."

He gave her a half smile and started the engine.

When they reached Pine Valley Mart, there were only a handful of cars in the parking lot. It seemed that the residents of this small town had other Friday night plans that didn't include grocery shopping.

As they walked into the grocery store, hand in hand, Nelson bypassed the carts. So he wasn't here for quantity, then.

She went along with him, up and down a couple of aisles, as Nelson seemed to be looking for something. He kept ahold of her hand, and she liked his intiative. It also made her realize that after tonight, when he dropped her off at her condo, there would be no more hanging out with Nelson. Holding hands. Kissing in a parking lot. Teasing each other.

Nelson stopped before a row of cleaning supplies. He picked up the Windex. "This reminds me of the color of your eyes."

She blinked.

His mouth curved. "I want to get you some things that remind me of you. Then you can get me things that remind you of me."

Her pulse thrummed with the way he was gazing at her. Like a guy who'd foolishly exposed his heart. "Okay . . ." she said in a quiet voice. "That's kind of bizarre, but sweet."

He only winked, then carried the Windex bottle with them as they continued down the aisle. Two aisles over, he stopped at the candy section. He picked up a bag of red cinnamon bears. "The color of your lips."

Lindsey was pretty sure she was blushing.

If he noticed, he didn't say anything.

They continued to another aisle, where Nelson picked up a spice jar of cinnamon. "Your freckles."

"You're kidding," she said with a laugh.

"Do I look like I'm kidding?" he asked, then he leaned down and placed a barely there kiss on her nose.

He led her by the hand to the next aisle, even though he was juggling the three things with his other hand.

"How far are you taking this?" she asked. "Do you need a cart?"

His gaze shifted to hers. "Yeah, that would be great. Ah." On the next aisle was an abandoned cart.

Nelson snagged it and loaded in the goods. "Perfect," he said.

When they reached the baking section, he picked up a jar of dark-chocolate frosting. "Like your hair."

"Really," Lindsey deadpanned.

He only grinned as he added the frosting to his collection. They ended up in the floral department a few minutes later, and Nelson proceeded to smell several of the arrangements. He also took the time to touch the petals.

"I don't think you're supposed to do that," Lindsey said.

"If you see someone coming, let me know," he answered.

Lindsey shook her head. "You're a nut. Besides, what will flowers remind you of?"

He picked up an arrangement of white tulips.

Her heart thumped as he crossed to her. Then he leaned down and said in her ear, "Your skin."

Lindsey swallowed. And blushed. And heated up all over.

Nelson turned and placed the tulips in the front of the cart.

When he looked over at her, she'd mostly composed herself.

"Now it's your turn," he said.

Lindsey wanted to drag him into some corner and kiss him. But she was a practical woman, and besides, once she started kissing him, she didn't know if she could end it there. "Okay, follow me," she said, although she had no idea what she was going to get yet.

They walked up and down a couple of aisles, the cart rattling as they went. Lindsey picked up a few things, acted like she was mulling them over, then put them back.

When they reached the meat section, Nelson said, "You'd better not."

She glanced over at him. "Better not *what*?"

"Get meat," he said. "To represent me."

"I'm not getting meat," Lindsey said. "Although you are kind of a meathead."

He grabbed her by the waist and hauled her into a bear hug.

Lindsey gasped, then laughed. "See what I mean?"

He released her with a chuckle, and she moved away from him because she was tempted to stay in his arms. She continued to the dairy section.

"Cheese?" he said when she picked up a block of cheese. "I think that's even worse."

Lindsey turned to face him, holding up the cheese. "Cheese gets better with age."

"So I'm an old man now?"

"No . . . the more time we spend together, the more I like you." She set the cheese into the cart. She felt his gaze on her as she walked through the dairy section.

When she reached the refrigerators of milk and dairy products, she heard a groan from Nelson.

She laughed. "It's not as bad as you think."

"You know I can't keep any of the fresh stuff," he said. The cart rattled closer. "I'll have to donate it to the bed and breakfast."

She picked up a carton of sour cream. "You when you're getting an MRI. As white as a ghost and kind of sour."

He scoffed and took the sour cream. He did the honors of putting the container into the cart. "Why don't you tell me what you really think of me?"

She only smiled and continued to walk, Nelson following with the rattling cart.

"I think I know why this cart was abandoned," he said in a wry tone.

She turned into the cereal aisle and stopped in front of the shelves of granola and protein bars. She picked up one that looked the gnarliest and the most full of protein. When she turned, Nelson had reached her spot.

"I'm planning on leaving anything made of seeds in Pine Valley," Nelson said.

"No seeds in this," she said. "Only gritty granola that's hard and tough like you, and if left on the counter without its wrapper, it will break your teeth."

Nelson grinned. "Okay, now we're getting somewhere." He leaned toward her, and she pressed the box against his chest.

Next, she led him back to the baking aisle, where she picked up a bag of marshmallows.

"I'm not sure I want to hear this," he said.

"You." She pointed at him. "On the inside. You've got a good heart, Nelson."

His gaze held hers, and she started to feel warm again. She set the marshmallows into the cart and continued walking until she reached the spice shelves. She took her time selecting what looked like a good BBQ seasoning. "To remember our first date."

He moved closer and grasped her hand.

Her heart was pounding like mad, and the way he was brushing his thumb over her wrist wasn't helping. "This is getting better."

She stepped back, tugging her hand away, but he wouldn't let go. They walked, hand in hand again, to the next aisle. Lindsey stopped in front of a section of tea and coffee choices. She picked up a silver-gray box that read Earl Gray.

"This reminds me of the color of your eyes," she said. Speaking of his eyes, they were 100 percent focused on her.

"I don't drink tea," he said.

"That's okay, because I do," she said. "Save it for me when I come visit you in Vegas."

His eyes searched hers. "You'll come see me in Vegas? You'd better not be messing with me, Lindsey Gerber."

She held back a smile. "I'm a lawyer, remember. I don't bullsh—"

"Language," he cut in, pressing a finger to her lips. "Remember, only positivity."

His finger was warm, like she knew the rest of him was. And she also knew that look in his eyes. "Don't."

His brows jutted. "Don't *what?*"

"Don't kiss me in the grocery store," she said.

He lowered his finger, then traced along her neck. Goose pimples raced across her skin.

"Why not?" he asked.

"Because it's tacky."

He smirked. "If you say so." He moved his hand behind her neck as he stepped closer.

She could hear him breathing, could practically hear his heart thumping. His smell of pine and rain seemed to wrap around her and push past any PDA reluctance. She lifted her hand and touched the scruff of his jaw, then traced the scar beneath his bottom lip.

The gray in his eyes seemed to burn right through her.

"Lindsey..." he whispered.

"Hello, folks," a deep voice crackled on the store's

intercom. "We're reminding you that our meat special this week is our ninety-eight percent lean hamburger for only two ninety-nine a pound."

Nelson stilled. "No one's in the store but us."

"I know, weird," she said. "It's almost like they want us to buy meat after all." She moved away from Nelson before he could grab her again.

Nelson laughed and followed her. "Now where are we going?"

"One more thing," she said, leading him to the automotive aisle. She chose a car freshener, pine scented. "To remind you of Pine Valley."

He took it from her and set it in the cart.

She moved away again and walked toward the front of the store. Nelson caught up with her in two strides and took her hand. She loved the warmth and strength she felt with his fingers linked through hers.

As the store employee rang up the items, Lindsey felt like the countdown had begun. Soon she'd say goodbye to Nelson. She wanted to look forward to visiting him in Vegas, but what if it didn't happen? It wouldn't surprise her if, once he returned to his team and his busy schedule, contact between them diminished. And she was already dreading the moment.

Fourteen

Nelson tossed his phone into his duffle bag, then shoved the bag into his locker. Lindsey's flight had been delayed.

Which meant she wouldn't be at the game tonight. After two weeks of not seeing her, Nelson didn't know if he could wait even a few hours longer. But it wasn't like he could drop everything and return to Pine Valley.

Tonight was their first playoff game, and every minute and second would count. If they won, then they'd continue to move up, and Coach would be on them every second. Which would make things a bit tricky with Lindsey visiting. Nelson hadn't told Coach that she was coming. He figured some of the other guys on his team had girlfriends, and two of them were married. In fact, Blaine was dealing with a long-distance relationship with a college girl at Belltown University, where he'd graduated. Belltown was all the way in Massachusetts. About as far from Vegas as a person could get.

Speaking of Blaine ... The halfback called to him, "Coach's meeting is starting now."

Nelson looked over to see that the locker room had cleared without him realizing, since he'd been caught up in his own disappointed thoughts about Lindsey's flight delay. The freak lightning storm in Northern California had better calm down soon.

"Thanks, man," Nelson told Blaine. "I'm on my way."

On game days, Coach wanted everyone at the ice arena hours before. They'd share a light meal, then listen to whatever speech Coach had prepared. After that, they'd go through stretches with the trainer before anyone suited in their hockey gear to warm up on the ice.

Nelson headed out of the locker room and slipped into the room with the buffet table set up. He got into the back of the line, right behind Blaine, without anyone noticing that he'd almost been late. Since the other guys were already sitting on the chairs with their cold-cut sandwiches, Nelson spoke to Blaine in a low voice. "Hey, can I ask you something personal?"

Blaine looked over at Nelson, surprise in his brown eyes. "Sure thing."

"With your, uh, girlfriend at Belltown," he said. "Is it hard to stay connected when you're so far apart?"

Blaine seemed to take the question in stride. "There are definitely days when I hate it, but we video chat a lot. She also comes out one weekend a month."

Nelson was surprised. He had no idea. Blaine hadn't ever missed any team events. "Really. And she's okay with that?"

Blaine smiled. "Well, she thinks I'm worth it, I guess. Besides, her scholarship at Belltown makes it a hard thing to pass up. Free education and all. She wants to be a physical therapist, and I'm only too happy to be her guinea pig."

Well, Nelson didn't want *those* kinds of details. "Thanks, dude."

Blaine hadn't moved forward in line during their conversation. "Can I ask why?"

"If things go well, you'll find out soon enough." Nelson stepped around him.

Blaine chuckled. "Someone you met while in Pine Valley?"

"Maybe," Nelson hedged, adding salad to his plate.

Blaine grinned. "I thought you were a little different when you returned. And it wasn't just the physical therapy."

Nelson lifted his gaze to meet Blaine's. "Different how?" Had Coach noticed? His other teammates?

Blaine lifted a shoulder. "Distracted. Staring at nothing when we're in meetings. Looking like a lovesick cow."

Nelson scoffed. "Whatever." But as he crossed the room to find a seat, he wondered if anyone else had noticed something different about him. He wished he could check his cell again and see if Lindsey had sent any flight updates.

He'd barely started to eat when Coach got up in front of the room. Nelson tried to pay attention, he really did. But he was thinking of Lindsey and if she'd make it to Vegas at all. If the flight was canceled, would she find another airline or stay in Pine Valley? What Nelson really wanted to ask Blaine was how *he* handled it. How he stayed busy and kept the game in his head.

Coach looked directly at Nelson and said, "Right, Nelson?"

Nelson blinked. He had no idea what Coach had just said. "Right," Nelson said.

That seemed to be good enough. Coach continued talking about visualization and how important it was to visualize the plays and outcome of the game before the game even started. Nelson had no problem doing that. Usually.

Right now, he was visualizing Lindsey texting him that

she wasn't coming to Las Vegas after all. Yeah, so maybe he was a lovesick cow. And it was really going to be miserable when he got to the end of tonight's game, and still no Lindsey.

Nelson suppressed a frustrated sigh, keeping his gaze focused on Coach even though the words weren't being registered.

Finally, Coach wrapped up with, "Find your quiet zone, men. Review what you know about the Chicago Flyers. Visualize how you, each one of you individually, will play like you've prepared to play. Each move, each shot, each block . . . they all count toward the whole."

The players clapped, Nelson included. He caught Ben's eye. Nelson sensed the second-string goaltender had been watching him during the entire meeting. But Nelson had been too caught up in his thoughts to notice. Nelson gave the guy a small nod, and Ben returned his gaze to Coach.

Meeting over, and Nelson rose and dumped the rest of his sandwich in the trash. He'd only been able to stomach about half of it. Which was . . . unusual. But he couldn't help thinking about how Lindsey had teased him for eating so much.

"You okay?" It was Minky. The huge forward was a brute on the ice, but off the ice, he was observant.

"Yeah, sure," Nelson said as the group of them headed out of the room. "How about you?"

Minky scoffed. "Don't try to avoid the question."

Nelson slowed his step so that the other players moved ahead of them, out of earshot. "I was hoping someone could come to the game tonight, that's all."

"Well, for your sake, I hope she makes it."

Nelson didn't have to ask why Minky would assume the person was a *she*. It seemed Nelson was pretty transparent.

An hour later, he stepped out onto the ice. There hadn't

been any more updates from Lindsey, and he decided he wasn't going to worry about it until his team had defeated the Flyers. Being back on the ice had felt good, but Blaine had been right. Things about Nelson had changed while he was in Pine Valley. Maybe it was that he took life a little more seriously. He'd also seen retirement staring him in the face with an injury taking him out for several weeks.

He wasn't ready to retire from the game he loved so much, but he was also looking beyond the game for the first time that he could ever remember.

Coach called out a drill to start with, and Nelson moved into the warm-up routine. His knee was feeling great, normal, but he was definitely aware of his movements more than ever. He tried not to favor it, because that had the potential to weaken his defense. So he had to steel his mind to pretend that he hadn't been injured in the first place.

After the first couple of drills, Nelson skated to the goalie box. Minky took shots at him, and Nelson blocked them one after another. Ben warmed up in the goalie box on the opposite side. In between shots, Nelson took a couple peeks at the stands to see if there was anyone he recognized. Not yet.

The other team was already prepping to come onto the ice, and the coaches were watching the warmups, collecting last-minute intel to use in their own strategies against each team.

Twenty minutes later, Nelson went to the bench with his team while the Chicago Flyers took their turn to go through their own warm-up drills.

Then it was time for the game to start. The arena was mostly filled. While the national anthem was sung, Nelson again checked the stands for Lindsey. He'd put a ticket on will-call, which would put her a few rows above the bench. Still, he didn't see her. And now the time had come when he couldn't think of anything but the game.

The first period started out fast and furious, with the Flyers' fullback colliding with Minky and sending him crashing to the ice. Minky got up as quickly as possible, but the Flyers were already past the center line and plowing through the Falcons as if their bodies were made of air.

Nelson was ready, though, and he deflected not one but two goalie shots. "Give me some defense!" he called to the fullbacks. "There's only one of me."

Five minutes into the first period, Nelson knew they were outmatched. Shot after shot got through the defense, and Nelson had deflected at least a dozen drives. It was going to be a long night. "Let's go, boys!" he called more than once.

During the short intermission between period one and two, Nelson drank his water and focused on Coach's instructions, mostly to the other players. Nelson didn't allow himself to check the stands again.

Second period started right off with Minky scoring on the Flyers. The Falcons' fans went nuts, and it was just the motivation they needed to turn the game in the Falcons' favor. Everyone on the team was hyper focused, and they were becoming the aggressors instead of the defenders.

When the second period ended, Nelson went to the bench with his teammates, feeling both elated and anxious about the upcoming third period.

"This is it," Coach said. "In seventeen minutes, we begin the third period. If you win this game, we're in the conference finals."

Nelson nodded. One more period. They could do this. When the warning buzzer went off, the team began to file out onto the ice.

"I think that lady's looking at you," Minky said. "Just above the bench." Minky continued to skate past Nelson to his position.

The words hit Nelson like a thunderbolt. He skated to the goal and turned to take his position. Only then did he allow himself to look.

Lindsey was sitting between two other people, and her cheeks were flushed a pretty pink. Whether from the coolness of the arena or something else, he didn't know. Her dark hair was waved about her shoulders in loose curls, and he wasn't sure if he'd ever seen her with curls. Then her gaze connected with his, and she smiled. It was like another thunderbolt.

She was even prettier than he remembered, and he had a good memory.

The ref skated to the center of the rink and dropped the puck between the two opposing forwards. Third period had officially started, and Nelson pulled his gaze from Lindsey. She was here. She'd made it. Somehow.

Minky made an aggressive drive and shot, but it was intercepted, and one of the Flyers was coming straight at Nelson, apparently having dodged every Falcon on the ice. Nelson was ready. He'd be damned if they lost, especially now that Lindsey had made it.

The puck sailed straight for the high corner, and Nelson moved to block it. The puck glanced off his shoulder, then pinged against the goal, bouncing back into play. Nelson didn't like how close that was. One more half centimeter, and the Flyers would have scored.

"Come on, Blaine," Nelson shouted at his teammate.

Blaine had taken control of the puck, but the intermission had somehow stirred the Flyers into a frenzy.

Nelson blocked another direct shot to the goal, going down on his knees. He didn't feel pain, or at least he wasn't sure, because the adrenaline was high. Finally, Minky had the puck, outmaneuvering the Flyers. "Shoot, Minky!" Nelson called. "Now!"

Minky sent the puck right between the goalie's knees just before they clamped together.

The arena went wild.

Falcons up by two, but the Flyers weren't finished yet.

Nelson kept his gaze on the one player who had been making breakthroughs all night. Sure enough, the Flyer came barreling toward the goal, fire in his eyes, nostrils flared. The guy wasn't slowing down, and Nelson skated backward the final foot.

A split second before it happened, Nelson knew the player was going to crosscheck him. But Nelson didn't try to block the blow, because there was still the puck to deflect. Nelson moved his gaze to the progress of the puck, and the second the other player slammed into him, Nelson got his hockey stick on the puck and sent it toward the half line.

The crowd cheered, and Nelson knew it was almost the end of the third period. Chances were pretty low that the Flyers would score two points to tie and push them into overtime, but stranger things had happened.

When the buzzer finally sounded, Nelson nearly sagged in relief. His teammates crowded around, smacking his shoulder. "It was Minky," Nelson said. "He scored the two goals."

When he reached the bench, Blaine slapped Nelson's back. "You saved our season about thirty times. I wonder if you set a new league record."

Nelson pulled off his helmet and face mask. "I don't know," he said, and he didn't really care right now. Because Lindsey was here.

He looked up into the stands, which were already clearing out. She was standing, her hands clasped together as if she'd been clapping. She was wearing dark jeans and a black hockey T-shirt that said *Falcons*. Something he'd mailed to her. And it fit quite well, if he were to make an assessment.

She waved when their gazes connected, and the congratulations surrounding Nelson faded into a distant buzz. Lindsey smiled a slow smile, and then she started down the bleachers toward the bench.

His teammates began to leave, but Nelson waited for Lindsey to make her way against the tide of the departing crowd. He unlaced his skates and tugged them off, then he opened the connecting half door and stepped out as she reached the bottom row. Lindsey was wearing high heels, which made Nelson chuckle.

"What's so funny?" she asked.

Her voice was much better in person. "Do you ever wear anything but high heels?" he asked.

"Only when moving boxes."

She continued toward him, which Nelson took as a good thing. Her blue eyes locked with his, and wow, it was so good to see her. He wanted to kiss her, but he was a sweaty mess, plus there were a lot of people around.

"That was some game, Mr. Goaltender," she said, folding her arms. "I mean, the two points were great, but you're the one who kept those points uncontested."

"I'm glad you could come," he said, keeping his voice low.

"Me too."

Okay, this was ridiculous. He had to get showered so that he could show her a proper greeting.

One of his teammates clapped him on the shoulder with a congratulations as he passed.

Nelson said, "Thanks, you too, man," without even looking to see who it was.

He couldn't take his eyes from Lindsey, but he was going to have to. "Can you meet me at that portal in about ten minutes? I've got to get showered and changed."

Lindsey did a slow perusal of his person, her lips quirked. "Ten minutes, huh? That quick?"

"Maybe nine."

She laughed, and Nelson stepped away. The longer he waited, the longer that ten minutes would be.

Fifteen

Waiting for Nelson at the portal he'd indicated had her stomach all tied up in knots. She'd thought he was a good-looking man before, but in his hockey gear ... Suffice it to say, she wasn't cold for a second in the chilled arena. But it wasn't just his personal appearance that had the butterflies growing; it was the way he'd acknowledged her. How his eyes had held hers. How he'd smiled. And asked her to wait for him.

She could tell he was happy to see her, and that made her even happier. And possibly crazy. She was in Vegas at a hockey game. *So* not her normal thing to do. Who would have thought that she, Lindsey Gerber, attorney at law, would be following a man around the country?

"Hey, you looking for someone?" a man said, passing by her, then slowing down.

He was about her age, tall, with brown eyes and black-as-night hair. He *had* to be a hockey player. For the Falcons or the Flyers, though?

"Uh, I'm waiting for Tyler Nelson."

The guy chuckled. "That so? He should be along in a minute."

"Are you... his teammate?"

"Yeah, I'm Blaine," he said, sticking out his hand.

She shook his rather large hand. "Lindsey."

He nodded, the smile still on his face. "Where you from?"

"Northern California."

"Ah," Blaine said in a knowing tone. "Nelson's questions make more sense now."

Well, this was interesting. Lindsey folded her arms. "What questions?"

Blaine took a step back, flashed another smile, and said, "I should probably shut up now. Nelson is bigger than me."

She was about to ask what size had to do with anything when she spotted Nelson coming down the long corridor.

"Gotta run," Blaine said, but Lindsey wasn't paying him attention any longer.

Nelson was striding toward her, a duffle bag slung over his shoulder. His fitted Henley shirt followed the ripples of his torso. And his jeans, well, they fit him perfectly too. Did he have a tailor? Or did clothing companies use his body for their measurements?

Breathe, Lindsey. He's just a guy. So what if he's the reason the Falcons are advancing to the conference finals? And he lives far from Pine Valley, so don't start creating what-if scenarios.

Someone called out to Nelson from behind him, and he turned and waved but continued walking toward Lindsey.

His gray eyes were dark, and his hair still damp from his shower.

She exhaled, then inhaled.

"Thanks for waiting," he said as he reached her.

She felt herself smiling when he dropped his duffle on the ground and pulled her into a hug.

She wrapped her arms about his neck and pressed her face against his skin. He smelled so good, like clean soap and Tyler Nelson. His body was warm, and his arms were holding her like he wasn't going to let go any time soon.

"I missed you, Lindsey Gerber," he said, his voice rumbling against her ear.

A warm shiver traveled the length of her body. She closed her eyes. "I missed you too, Tyler Nelson."

His hold only tightened, but Lindsey didn't mind. Reality would hit her soon enough—the reality of the impossibility of their situation. She pushed all worries and questions from her mind and focused on breathing in this warm, strong man who was working his way into her heart.

When he finally drew away, Lindsey wanted to pull him close again, but she was an adult woman. Not some infatuated teenager with her crush. She released Nelson, already dreading when she'd have to get on that return flight out of Vegas.

Nelson picked up his duffle, slung it over his shoulder in a smooth motion, then grasped her hand. "My truck's through here." He led her down the corridor toward an exit. "How long was the flight delayed?"

"About an hour," she said as he pushed through the exit door. "But the pilot made good time, and the flight was shorter than expected. So here I am."

He stopped beneath one of the parking lot streetlamps and looked down at her. "Here you are."

The intensity of his gaze and the depth of his voice sent a new round of flutters through her. He leaned down, his eyes still on her, then he pressed his mouth against hers. It wasn't like their other parking lot kiss. This one was more of an icebreaker.

Nelson's mouth was warm and possessive, even though he wasn't holding her. In fact, he wasn't touching her at all, just his mouth against hers.

She wanted to twine her arms about his neck again, but she decided it would be wise to keep this public kiss as hands off as possible.

Nelson drew away much too soon, but his gaze remained. "Hungry?" he asked.

"Yeah," she said. "I haven't eaten all day." It was probably not something she should have admitted. Too late now.

His brows lifted. "Why not?"

"Nerves, I guess." She shrugged. "I might be your match and eat more than you tonight."

His gaze moved down the length of her body. "I doubt it. But I'm not going to stop you from trying." He pulled a key fob from his pants pocket and clicked on it. Not far from where they stood, the headlights of a truck flashed.

"Come on," he said. "I'm starving too."

He opened the passenger side of the truck for her, and she climbed into the seat. The truck was clean and smelled like him, which only made her belly flutter again. Sitting in a man's vehicle always told her a bit about him. There was a Falcons jacket in the back seat and a couple of empty sports-drink bottles.

Hanging from the rearview mirror was a pine-scented car freshener. And Lindsey had the feeling it was the one she'd given him. After he walked around the truck, he tossed the duffle bag into the back seat, then climbed in.

He started the engine, then turned to her. "Why are you nervous?"

She hadn't expected the question, so her answer wasn't filtered. "About you, about your game, about coming here." She winced. "That about covers it."

He gazed at her for a moment, then took her hand and drew it to his lips. After placing a kiss on the back of her hand, he said, "If it makes you feel any better, I'm nervous too."

She gave a half laugh. "Why?"

"Because it's been two weeks since I last saw you, and I didn't know what it was going to be like seeing you again," he said. "I didn't know how I'd feel . . . or if I'd still feel the same as I did in Pine Valley."

Her heart skipped at least one beat, possibly three or four. "And how do you feel now?" she ventured to say, even though they probably shouldn't be having *this* talk only a short time after their reunion.

"Hooked."

"*Hooked?*"

"Yeah, hooked." He was still holding her hand, and he brushed his thumb over the outside of her wrist ever so slowly. "I'm no lawyer or wordsmith, so the only way I can describe how I feel about you is *hooked.*"

Thankfully the dimness in the cab of the truck hid Lindsey's blush. "You're a decent wordsmith. Don't sell yourself short."

He smiled. "Then you don't feel nervous, okay? Remember I'm hiding all of those flaws."

"Ha. Ha."

He squeezed her hand before letting go and putting the truck into reverse. After backing out and shifting into drive, he grasped her hand again.

"Do you like Chinese food?" he asked as he turned out of the parking lot and pulled onto the road.

"Sure."

Nelson picked up his phone, then spoke into the Bluetooth. "Chinese restaurant near me." The video screen on his dash glowed to life, and Nelson called the Chinese place through the voice-prompt system. After ordering more than enough food, he hung up.

"I thought we could eat at my place, you know, uninterrupted by a server or other people," he said. "In Vegas, I get recognized a lot."

"All your adoring fans will be disappointed," Lindsey teased. "Or you don't want me to get jealous of all the fawning ladies?"

He chuckled, then his tone turned serious. "I'm not a player, Lindsey."

"I know."

He seemed surprised at this. "You *know*?"

"Don't forget my profession, Nelson," she said. "I'm pretty good at research."

"So, what, you did a background check?"

Maybe she shouldn't admit so much, but if he couldn't take the heat and the scrutiny . . . "Yeah, among other things. And it's not something I do with every man I go out with, I'll have you know."

"I'm a special case?"

She couldn't read his tone, but he was still holding her hand, so there was that. "I was flying out to meet you, and a woman's gotta do her due diligence."

"I get it," he said. "I'm glad you did. I'd hope my sister would do the same before flying around the country to watch some guy's hockey game." He pulled into a condo complex and drove past the first building, then parked in a numbered space.

The palm trees and lighting from the streetlamps made the place look like a postcard.

As they walked to his condo, he said, "Where did you decide to stay?"

"A hotel by the airport," she said. "I sent my luggage with the hotel shuttle."

They stopped in front of a door, and Nelson unlocked it. As he pushed open the door and flipped on an interior light, he said, "You know I have plenty of room. And an extra bedroom."

"I know, you told me," she said, ignoring how the timbre of his suggestion was still tempting, even though she'd already said no.

Lindsey walked into the condo. It was plainer than she'd imagined, not that she knew what to expect in the first place. The front room had the standard leather couch and a square coffee table with a few magazines scattered across it. All of them looked like hockey or other sports magazines.

A black-and-white painting on the wall drew her attention. It was an abstract, and the slashes and swirls didn't seem to take any form or represent something.

"Have a seat," Nelson said. "I'll put my stuff away."

She moved to the couch and sat down. From her position, she could see into the dim kitchen, where she spotted a black-painted table and four chairs. Nothing was on the counters. That surprised her the most. It was almost like he didn't live here. She didn't know what she'd expected exactly, but maybe he had a house in another city? Her investigation had also revealed that Nelson's pro-hockey salary made him a millionaire many times over.

Nelson was moving about in another room, then Lindsey heard the sound of rushing water. He'd started a laundry load, and she guessed it was stuff he'd worn tonight. The domesticity of it all made her feel fluttery again. Which was ridiculous. Just because he was an amazing hockey player and had plenty of money didn't mean he couldn't do his own laundry.

The doorbell rang, and Lindsey rose to her feet as Nelson came down the hall.

"Must be the food." He passed her, then opened the door and paid for the giant bags of food.

Once the delivery man left, Nelson turned to her. "Hope you're as hungry as you said you are."

"It smells great." She followed him into the kitchen, and while he grabbed some water bottles from the fridge, she pulled the containers from the bag.

"Do you want a fork?" Nelson asked. "Or there should be chopsticks in one of the sacks."

"I'll manage with the chopsticks."

Nelson nodded. "Great, I'll do that too."

Lindsey opened the containers. Her stomach was grumbling, and she'd have to make herself eat slow.

She picked up chicken from the cashew-chicken container. It was really good. She dug in again and ate some more.

"Like it?" Nelson asked. He hadn't touched any of the food but was leaning back in his chair, watching her.

"I do." She pointed her chopsticks at him. "Aren't you going to eat?"

"I'm enjoying watching you eat."

She made a face and pushed the container of cashew chicken toward him. "Try this. You'll like it."

Nelson smiled, then leaned forward and picked up his chopsticks. "Yes, ma'am."

Sixteen

It wasn't that Nelson couldn't use chopsticks. In theory. He had the basics down, but Lindsey seemed quite at ease, whereas he had to try two or three times to get in a single bite.

"You can use a fork; I won't judge you," Lindsey said, laughter in her tone.

Nelson met her blue gaze over his kitchen table. He was still sort of in awe that she was *here*, in Vegas, and in his condo. She looked good in his condo too. A nice contrast to the plain black-and-white surroundings. He wasn't much of a decorator, and save for the one abstract painting hanging on the living room wall, he hadn't added anything since moving in.

"I can manage with chopsticks," Nelson said. "I'm sure it gets easier with practice, like everything else."

Lindsey was obviously trying not to laugh at him. "Whatever you say." She took another bite of the chow mein. She made eating with chopsticks look easy.

He fumbled with his next bite but was finally victorious. He wasn't going to get full any time soon eating this way. "Is there anything you *can't* do, Lindsey Gerber?"

She didn't hesitate. "I can't play hockey. I can't even ice skate."

"Everyone can ice skate," he said. "When's the last time you went?"

"Um, never."

He stared at her, and she stared right back. "You're kidding," he said finally.

"Nope." She shrugged and speared some of the sweet-and-sour pork.

"We're going ice skating tomorrow."

"We really don't have to," she said. "Aren't you on the ice enough?"

"Not with you."

She shook her head. "You're a nut, and I'm getting you a fork."

Before Nelson could protest, Lindsey stood and grabbed a fork from one of the drawers. She brought it over to him.

"Why, thank you."

Lindsey smirked. "No, I'm the one who's thankful. It's painful to watch you eat a bite about every five minutes."

He chuckled, then started eating like he usually did. With a fork. He looked up a few moments later to find Lindsey watching him. "You were right, happy?"

She only smiled.

When they'd both finished, Lindsey started packing up the containers and setting them on the counter. As she opened the fridge, Nelson said, "Let's just throw those away."

Lindsey looked down at the container in her hands. "It will still be good for a couple of days."

He took the container. "I don't eat leftovers."

Lindsey looked from him to the inside of the fridge, which he knew was basically filled with water bottles and sports drinks. "You really don't eat leftovers? Why not?"

"Because that's what I grew up on," he said, bypassing Lindsey and closing the fridge door. "Fast-food leftovers. And I decided that the day I could afford to eat freshly prepared meals, I'd stop eating leftovers."

Lindsey took the container back, opened the fridge, and set it on the middle shelf. Then she proceeded loading every single container that still held food into the fridge.

Nelson watched her, arms folded.

When she faced him, she was smiling. "I love leftovers. In fact, I think sometimes the food is better the second time around. So if I'm hanging out with you tomorrow, I want to know that I can open your fridge and warm up some delicious Chinese food."

She made a good argument. A dang good one.

"Tell you what," he said. "You come over here and kiss me with that sassy mouth of yours, and the leftovers can stay in the fridge."

"Told you your insides are like marshmallows," she said, moving closer to him.

He unfolded his arms, and she ran her hands up his chest.

Yeah. It was good to have her in Vegas, in person.

Her hands continued their path, moving over his shoulders, then to the edges of the collar of his shirt. She smelled of that perfume she always wore.

He grasped her hips and pulled her close.

Lindsey only smiled, then she moved her hands behind his neck and into his hair. When she finally kissed him, he closed his eyes and kissed her back.

They kissed slowly at first. But the heat steadily built, and Nelson moved his hands up her back, anchoring her against him. Her curves melded against the planes of his body, and he marveled at how perfectly they seemed to fit together.

He drew back to breathe, only to lean down and kiss the side of her neck, then lower. Lindsey sighed and gripped his shoulders as he kissed her collar bone. Her skin was soft, like the petals of the tulips he'd given her in Pine Valley, her scent intoxicating, and her hands on him created an existence he never wanted to return from.

"Nelson," she whispered.

He was lost, though, in her touch, in her taste, and it wasn't until she said his name louder that he lifted his head.

Her cheeks were flushed pink, her lips swollen from their kissing. "We need to cool things off." Her gaze was both serious and amused.

So he kissed her gently on the mouth. "Are you sure? I'm kind of enjoying this."

She moved a hand along his neck, then over his shoulder, and stopping at his bicep. "I don't want things to move too fast, because I really like you."

"Isn't that an oxymoron?" His mind was starting to return to earth, but only just.

Lindsey bit her bottom lip.

Not helping.

"I don't want to mess things up between us," she said. "You know, make it all about the physical stuff. I can't deny that I'm tempted to stay here tonight, but . . ."

He traced the edge of her jaw with his thumb. "I do know," he murmured. "Because I feel the same way. Lindsey Gerber, you're not a fling. And I hope that you don't think I see you that way."

She didn't respond for a moment, then she pulled him into a hug.

Nelson held her close. It seemed like with every interaction with Lindsey, he was falling deeper and deeper.

All for You

"Now what?" she murmured.

He chuckled. "Now what do we do since you made me stop kissing you?"

She drew away and smiled. "Yeah."

He pretended to think. "Well, there aren't any elk nearby to go watch. There's always the Strip, but I'd rather hang out with just you. We already ate. And the ice-skating rink is closed by now. So that leaves . . ."

"Not grocery shopping."

"Ha. No." He grasped her hand and drew her toward the living room. "Mindless movie watching while I try to steal more kisses."

Lindsey scoffed but let him lead her to the couch. He flipped on the big screen on the opposite wall, then pulled up a movie menu.

"You choose," he said, handing over the remote.

"Oh, no," she said, refusing to take it. "I chose last time, and we didn't even make it through the show. You're choosing."

"Okay." He scrolled through some of the genres, then settled on a Matt Damon flick that had come out about a year ago. "You want popcorn or anything?"

"I'm good," Lindsey said. "Do you even have popcorn?"

"No."

She laughed. "So what were you going to do, run to the store?"

"Start texting my neighbors."

Lindsey shook her head in amusement.

"I'll be right back," he said, and he returned to the kitchen to put together a bag of ice for his knee.

When he settled next to Lindsey and set the ice over his knee, she said, "Are you hurting?"

"Just sore," he said. And it was true, mostly. His knee

hadn't bothered him until he'd taken off his skates; of course, that was when the adrenaline from the game had started to wear off too.

"Well, you have three days until the conference finals, right?"

"Yeah," he said.

She nodded. "I read up on the Stanley Cup. I didn't know there could be seven games. I thought it was just one game."

"It's like the World Series, four out of seven games."

"Well, I'm sure your team is glad you're back," she said.

He should have agreed, because in theory it should be true, but returning after an injury was a lot tougher than he'd thought. He had to focus even more to keep his mental game, because he knew how easy it was now to tear something. And the glaring discontentment among some of the teammates was more obvious now that he'd been away from it for a few weeks.

Lindsey was gazing at him, small lines between her brows. "Aren't you glad to be back? I mean, tonight was an incredible game."

"Yeah." He lifted a hand and curled her hair around his fingers. "I just didn't know that I'd meet such an amazing woman who lived hundreds of miles away."

The edges of her mouth lifted. "No amazing women in Vegas?"

"Nope."

She laughed. And he smiled.

"So, I have some good news," she said. "I was going to tell you earlier, but we weren't done basking in your glory."

"And we're done now?" he teased.

She leaned close and kissed him on the cheek. How could such a small gesture make his pulse go wild?

"So, Paul dropped his personal suit," she said, "and

Dawson is pretty sure it's because he was put on long-term leave by the firm."

"Wow."

"*Unpaid* leave," she continued. "Apparently Paul the lawyer doesn't want to pony up lawyer fees."

"What about your case against the firm?"

"They want to negotiate a settlement, keep it out of the public eye."

"I can see pros and cons to that," Nelson said. "Pros are that it's going to be over a lot quicker, and you can move on with your life. Cons are that paying a settlement feels like a mere slap."

Lindsey scooted closer to him and wrapped her arms about his waist. Then she nestled her head against his shoulder. "That's what I like about you, Nelson. Sometimes I feel like you can read my mind."

He wrapped his arms around her. "Not too bad for a meathead."

She only held him tighter.

"So what are you going to do?"

"I don't know yet," she said. "Dawson and I are going over everything on Tuesday. I told him I needed a few days to think through everything."

"Do you want me to come to that meeting?" he asked.

She drew away and looked at him. "You can't leave Vegas. What would your coach say? Besides, the semis are Monday night. What are the chances of there being a late flight?"

"I'll charter a plane," he said.

When she shook her head, he added, "I'm not exactly on a tight budget, despite the sparseness of my condo. Thanks to my sister's advice, I've been pretty good about investing."

"You don't have a bunch of houses you haven't told me about?" she asked. "Or a secret gambling addiction?"

"Some property investments, but no houses," he said. "And I don't gamble ... which is probably a good thing, considering where I currently live."

"Still, you can't spend that kind of money on this—on *me*," Lindsey said. "I mean, your priority is your team. Your season."

"Priorities can change." The more he thought about it, the more he wanted to be in the meeting with Lindsey. To support her in whatever she needed.

Lindsey blinked. "You're making me nervous again." She placed her hand on his chest. "You're sweet to offer, but you need to be here with your team. I can Skype you in or something."

"Not the same."

She looped her arms about his neck. "I know. But I'm saying no." She kissed him then, and he didn't feel like he'd been let down at all.

Seventeen

Lindsey held onto the wall edging the ice-skating rink with an iron grip. She couldn't even walk in the ice skates Nelson had rented for her, let alone skate. And she was pretty sure she'd wrenched her ankle a dozen times. They hurt, her toes were pinched, and she was cold.

But Nelson seemed to be enjoying every minute of it.

"Come on," he said, skating toward her again, then slowing down. He grasped her by the waist, and she clung to his arms so she wouldn't lose her balance. Again.

"Just hold onto me," he said close to her ear.

The kids at the rink—kids who could not be more than four years old—were skating about like miniature Olympic ice skaters. Theoretically, if they could do it, she could too, right?

Nelson skated backwards, pulling her with him, and it was all she could do to stay upright. She held onto his arms, and her skates glided forward, but she felt as stiff as a board.

"You need to move your feet," he said. "Sort of like walking, but pushing away from the ice at the same time."

She tried, but a skate slipped out.

"I've got you," he said, keeping her upright. He was trying not to laugh, that she was sure of. "Bend your knees a little. That's the way."

Her skating wasn't improving. A few steps, then she was losing her balance again. "I think I'm good," she said, breathless, although she'd barely exercised. "I'll just watch you from that nice bench over there."

Nelson chuckled. "What? You think I'm going to put on a figure-skating show?"

"You can do whatever you want on the ice," she said. "I'm happy to watch. I won't feel left out, I promise."

A seven-year-old girl whizzed past them.

Lindsey sighed. Maybe if she'd taken up ice skating as a kid, she would be half decent at this.

"Look at me," Nelson said. "Focus on my face and relax. Don't worry about anyone else. Let your body get used to the feel of being on ice."

Lindsey shifted her gaze to his gray eyes. She loved his eyes. And she loved the way he was gazing at her. With affection and amusement—and it was like she could feel how much he cared about her from how he looked at her.

"You can breathe too," he said. "And although I don't mind you holding onto my arms, your nails are kind of sharp."

"Oh, sorry." She relaxed her grip, but only a tad. "Maybe you should have worn your protective hockey gear to save yourself from desperately clinging women."

Nelson did laugh then.

"I think I'm craving hot chocolate," she tried again.

"Twice around, that's all I ask."

It was hard to say no to the pleading in his eyes. "Okay, twice. Starting from the place you found me. So that'd be at least halfway already done, right?"

"Deal," he said. "Now, keep doing what you're doing, but let go of one of my arms. You choose which arm."

She exhaled, then lowered her left hand.

"See, you're doing great," he said.

"That's because you're still holding onto me."

"Keep on skating," he said, releasing her waist, then linking their hands. "Let go of my other arm."

She did. Now they were only holding hands, and she was still skating.

Another kid whizzed past her, but she kept her focus of putting one foot in front of the other.

"Okay, we're going to speed up a little," Nelson said. "You'll realize it's easier to skate when you're going faster."

"Not too fast," Lindsey said immediately.

He chuckled. "At your pace."

And before she realized it, they'd skated twice around the arena.

"Do you want to try once on your own?" he asked, slipping his hand from hers.

"Wait."

But he'd already let go and was skating in front of her now, backwards. "You're fine," he said. "Your feet and body have the rhythm down already. Just go with it."

She still felt wobbly, but she was skating, on her own, without holding onto anything. It was an exhilarating feeling. The cool air brushing past her, the smooth ice beneath her feet, the feeling of her body gliding. Then falling.

Nelson nearly caught her, but she hit the ice before anything could be done.

She sat on her rear, stunned for a moment. "Are you laughing?"

"I'm not laughing."

He was laughing.

She grasped his outstretched hand. "Now can I get hot chocolate?" she asked after he pulled her to her feet.

"The most important thing about ice skating is to get back up and keep skating after you've fallen," he said.

Lindsey peered up at him. "You sound like a meme."

He grinned. "Come on, I won't let go. But you've gotta shake it off."

She held onto his hand, maybe tighter than necessary, as they skated another round. When he led her off the ice, she said, "I don't think I've ever been so happy to get hot chocolate."

Nelson squeezed her hand, then they walked over to the bench. Well, Lindsey wobbled.

She sat down with a sigh. "I should have taken it up when I was about eight. Those kids out there are amazing."

"Don't cut yourself short," Nelson said. "You're ten times better now than when you first stepped on the ice. Besides, it's not like you don't have other skills and talents."

"True." She tugged at the knot of the laces on one of her ice skates. "We can't all be pro hockey players or seven-year-old ice-skating prodigies."

"Here, I'll get those off for you," he said, grasping her ankle. "What did you do, triple knot the laces?"

"I didn't want them to fall off," she said.

Nelson shook his head, but he was smiling. "You have these tied so tight, I don't think they would have come off if someone tried to yank them."

Lindsey watched Nelson work the laces loose on her ice skates. Warmth rushed to her cramped feet, almost painful, but a relief all the same.

When Nelson had patiently untied her second skate, he tugged off her socks that she'd had to buy from the rink. Then he turned to his own skates and had them off in mere seconds. Well, he *was* a professional.

Lindsey buckled on the wedge sandals that she'd worn to the rink and stood from the bench. Immediately, she grasped the wall in front of her. "Oh wow. This feels weird." She felt like she was walking on a moving surface.

"Give it a few seconds," Nelson said, grasping her hand again. "I think hot chocolate will make it even better."

After they returned the skates and Lindsey threw away the purchased socks, they headed to the snack bar. Lindsey wished she weren't flying out that night. She was already missing him. His coach had called a second practice today, so in a couple of hours, they'd say goodbye.

Coming to Vegas had only solidified that she liked Nelson very much. And she wanted to spend more time with him. If there was any point in her career that was flexible with time, this was it. But she didn't want to be burned down the road because of not putting in enough effort now.

Nelson had told her the first two games in the conference finals would be in Vegas. Then games three and four would be in Florida. If there was a game five, it would be back in Vegas. Lindsey would see how the next few days went, then maybe she'd return to Vegas for game two.

And she didn't think Nelson would mind, because he was currently watching her from across the little table they were sitting at near the snack bar.

"What?" she said, trying not to smile. The hot chocolate was definitely doing its job and beginning to thaw her out.

"Nothing," he said.

"You're staring at me."

He smirked. "I'm just wondering what you're thinking about."

"Isn't that what the woman is supposed to say?"

"I'm not a conventional guy," Nelson said.

Lindsey couldn't agree more. "A woman's got to have her secrets, you know."

Nelson nodded, but she could see that he clearly didn't agree. He sipped his hot chocolate. "So what do you want to do for our countdown?"

"Countdown?"

"You know, until I have practice and you have to leave."

"Are you hungry?" she asked.

"Always, but I can't eat a lot before a practice."

Lindsey smiled. "Then let's go somewhere to eat that's light." They didn't have time for a movie, and if they went back to his place, she knew they'd probably just end up on the couch kissing and trying not to cross too many lines.

As they headed out of the rink and across the parking lot to his truck, Lindsey tried not to wince at the pain in her feet. She was pretty sure she'd have blisters.

"Are you okay?" Nelson asked, observant as always.

"Yeah," she said. "Next time I'll have to go one size up on the ice skates."

He used his key fob and unlocked the truck, then opened the passenger door for her.

When he climbed in the other side, he didn't start the engine but said, "Let me see your feet."

"What? Why?"

"So I can rub them out."

Lindsey felt the heat rush to her face. "You can't do that."

"Why not?" He seemed sincere.

"Seriously, they probably stink, and—"

He grasped her calf and hauled her leg up on the seat.

She was too stunned to protest anymore. So she turned more toward him.

Nelson unbuckled her wedge sandal on her left foot, then set the shoe on the seat. He began to rub her foot, gently.

Lindsey could only stare. And blush. She'd never had a guy do something like this for her. It was . . . intimate . . . and it felt amazing.

"If I'm hurting you, let me know," he said, glancing up at her.

"Not hurting," she said.

He smiled, then looked down again to resume his work.

Lindsey sighed and relaxed as much as possible in her position. "You're a man of many talents, Tyler Nelson. Are you a part-time masseuse or something?"

The edge of his mouth lifted. "No, I've had my feet rubbed out many times by trainers, so I know a few things."

Boy, he sure knew those few things well. His very capable fingers moved from the top of her foot to her ankle. Lindsey was insanely glad she'd shaved and that her last pedicure had only been a few days ago. Although she still worried a little about the odor. But Nelson didn't seem bothered, and in truth, she couldn't smell anything.

He picked up her other leg and unbuckled her shoe.

Lindsey exhaled, the butterflies in her stomach doing nosedives.

Nelson started on the other foot, and it was as if her body knew what was coming. Heat traveled from where he was touching her all the way up her leg and into her body. There was no denying it. Tyler Nelson was probably the sexiest man she knew. And he was caring. Generous. And for some reason he liked *her*, enough to rub out her sore feet after she'd whined for an hour while they ice skated.

Nelson stopped with the foot rub all too soon, yet it was a good thing he had, because Lindsey's resolve to stay away from his apartment had all but disappeared.

To top everything off, he put her shoes back on, and when he struggled with the tiny buckle, she leaned forward and finished. She slid her feet to the bottom of the truck and moved closer to Nelson.

"Thank you," she said, and she looped her arms about his neck.

His gray gaze held hers as he said, "You're welcome," in a soft tone.

Lindsey didn't think any woman in her right mind could blame her for kissing Nelson then. He definitely deserved her gratitude, and right now, this was how she was going to express it.

Nelson slipped his arms around her waist and pulled her closer as he kissed her back. "I guess now I know what you like," he murmured in a raspy voice.

She smiled. "Any time you're in the mood to rub my feet, I'm happy to oblige."

"Like right now?" he said, his breath warm against her neck.

She ran her fingers through his hair, then across the back of his neck. His skin was warm, and when her fingers moved to his jaw, she traced the whiskers there that he hadn't shaved this morning. "I'm taking like five rainchecks," she said. "Because I'd rather eat with you than in the airport or on the plane."

The edges of his mouth lifted, then he kissed her again. "Okay, babe, let's go then."

She'd always thought the term *babe* was cheesy, but when Nelson said it to her, she only heard affection. And she was not going to complain about it, ever.

Nelson released her to start the truck, and she only moved over a few inches to give him room to drive. Her feet did feel amazingly better, and every pinch of the ice skates and her multiple falls had been worth *this*.

Eighteen

Monday morning's practice had been light, in preparation for the game that night against the Florida Ducks. But Nelson found himself in the training room, an ice bag strapped to his knee. Thankfully everyone, including Coach, had already left, so it was just Nelson and the team trainer, Riley.

"There's some swelling," Riley said with a frown as he felt around Nelson's knee after the first fifteen minutes of ice.

"It's not hurting, though." *Much.* Yeah, there was some achiness, and Nelson wanted to protect his knee as much as possible. "That's good, right?"

"It's good," Riley confirmed, but his tone was tight. "One more ice pack, then you can get home and rest."

Nelson dropped his head back onto the padded table while Riley strapped the second ice pack to his knee. Rest? He'd had too much rest in Vegas. In fact, he'd done less since getting back into the season than he had in Pine Valley with

Maddy. Tonight was the first game in the conference finals. Hopefully they'd win four right out of the gate, then they'd go straight to the Stanley Cup.

Once they got through the Stanley Cup, Nelson was going to take a full month off—in Pine Valley. He wouldn't tell Coach until it was necessary. And he wasn't going to tell Lindsey yet. If things kept progressing with her, he wanted to spend more time with her than phone calls and a day here and there. He wanted to get to know her better, because he wanted to know if he could trust his instincts.

Instincts that made it clear his life was moving in a direction that he hadn't planned . . . at least hadn't thought could happen for years. Nelson didn't know if he was in love with Lindsey, but so far, it was the closest he'd ever come. He liked everything about her, and he supposed that he might be blinded by his own attraction to her to overlook any flaws—which of course existed. But nothing that he could pick out or potentially see as a deal-breaker. Except for maybe where she lived.

Nelson exhaled slowly. Lindsey living in Pine Valley was definitely a barrier, but not impossible, right?

A timer went off, and Nelson opened his eyes.

Riley walked back to the table. "Keep me posted on how you're feeling," he said. "I can come in early tonight if you need me."

"I will," Nelson said, moving to a sitting position.

Riley pulled off the ice bag, and Nelson got off the table. His knee was numb enough that he didn't feel the earlier achiness, only a cold ache now.

He picked up his duffle from one of the benches, then headed out of the training room and locker area. Once in his truck, he turned his cell phone on. Several texts chimed through. The first one he saw was from his sister, wishing him luck and saying she'd be coming to game two on Wednesday night.

The next text was from Lindsey, continuing the flirty text banter they'd been engaged in before practice, in which they were trying to guess each other's biggest flaw.

Lindsey's earlier text had read: *You don't keep any leftovers, so in essence you're wasting money that could be put to good use somewhere else.*

Nelson had no problem defending himself. *I'm fairly skilled at knowing how much I'll eat, so I rarely have leftovers in the first place. Besides, I thought you were starving the other night. Maybe your big flaw is that you like to tell people what to do.*

Lindsey had sent a laughing emoji, then wrote: *Only if they need direction. Which I think you have plenty of.*

So it's not a flaw? he'd written.

Not for you, she'd replied.

Now it had been a couple hours since her last text, and he wrote, *I've had time to think about what your real flaw must be.*

The three dots in the texting app danced, and he smiled. She must not be too swamped to reply right away.

Don't hold me in suspense, big guy.

Nelson smiled. *You haven't made plans to come to Vegas again.*

No reply for two full minutes, and Nelson wondered if he'd blown it. She knew he couldn't go to Pine Valley—it wasn't an option until after the Stanley Cup, if the team got that far. But when he'd taken her to her hotel last Saturday, they hadn't really committed to a next time.

The three dots jumped, indicating she was writing back. Nelson stared at his phone screen, hoping that he hadn't screwed up by presuming too much. She was plenty busy, and he couldn't expect . . .

What makes you think I don't already have plans to come to Vegas?

His pulse jumped, and he couldn't stand it any longer. He pressed SEND on her number.

When she answered, he could hear the smile in her voice. "Are you messing with me, Lindsey Gerber?" he asked.

"When have I ever messed with you, Tyler Nelson?"

Hearing her voice only made him miss her more. "Right now," he said. "This exact moment. You're messing with my mind and my heart."

"I really don't mean to mess with your heart," she said in a teasing voice, "but your mind is fair game."

Nelson groaned. "Just tell me your plans."

"How about I tell you my plans after you win tonight's game?"

"And if we don't win," he said in a slow voice, "will you still tell me your plans?"

"You really need to be focusing on your upcoming conference-playoff game, Mr. Goaltender," she said. "If you win, then I'll let you know."

"You're killing me, babe."

"Focus, Nelson, focus," she said.

"Then stop being so distracting."

She laughed, and Nelson grinned like the fool he was. He'd make sure his team won the game tonight.

"Okay, I really should go," she said. "I think my new client just parked in front of the building."

"I'm calling you later, and you'd better have the information I want."

"Whatever, mobster," she said, a smile in her voice before they hung up.

Nelson leaned his head back on the headrest. Maybe he'd be seeing Lindsey a lot sooner than he'd anticipated. He could only hope.

Three hours later, he was back at the arena. He drove past the line that had already formed at the front doors, with spectators wearing Florida Ducks and Vegas Falcons gear alike. As he climbed out of his truck, he was feeling confident, good, and strong. All where he needed to be in his head.

Minky's BMW came through the parking lot, and he made a sharp turn into a space, squealing the tires of his car.

Nelson shook his head.

Minky climbed out, a grin on his face. "Did you hear that?"

"Any time you want to race, I'm in," Nelson said.

The two men clapped backs in a bro hug.

"Well, this is it," Minky said. "You ready to bring the heat?"

"More than ready," Nelson said. "I wish this were the Stanley Cup."

Minky laughed. "Yeah, let's get through the Ducks first."

"Quack, quack," Nelson said.

They both aimed fake rifles and said "Boom" at the same time. The joke was juvenile, but it still made both of them laugh.

"Are we expecting a certain female spectator tonight?" Minky asked.

"Not tonight," Nelson said.

"Pouting?" Minky nudged him.

Nelson shoved him back. "Shut up."

Minky laughed and opened the side door that led to the locker room. The security guard stationed inside the door waved them through.

Minky teased him some more, but Nelson was hardly paying attention. He had to visualize the game and remember all the game film he'd watched on the Ducks. Winning game one of the conference finals would be a good omen for the rest of the games. By the time they'd dressed, gone into Coach's meeting, then warmed up on the ice, Nelson was more than ready.

The game was swift and furious, and the Falcons won, three to one.

The goal that had gotten past Nelson bothered him because it shouldn't have happened. But Nelson had been a split second too slow with his hockey stick. He knew that he'd remember the image the rest of the night and into the next day, until the Wednesday game would replace it with new images.

But he was happy for the win.

"Nice job, man," Blaine said, slapping him on the shoulder as they headed for the locker room to shower and change. Coach had also commissioned them to go into one of the portals and sign shirts and other fan gear.

Nelson needed to ice his knee, but if he stayed behind, then Coach would know something was up. So he showered and dressed and went out to sign autographs.

Anything that would help pass the time before he saw Lindsey again.

Nineteen

Lindsey didn't want to get out of bed. Not yet. Her blankets were just the right amount of cozy, and her body felt deliciously relaxed. It might also have something to do with the sweet conversation she'd had with Nelson last night after his team had won their game. Or her reluctance to climb out of bed might come from the fact that Nelson had just texted her again.

Are you awake yet, beautiful?

She sighed with giddiness as she read the words. Yeah, Nelson was kind of a sweet-talker, but as long as it was directed toward her, she didn't mind.

I'm awake, she texted. *I'm surprised you're not sleeping in.* It was 7:30 a.m.

I guess I'm too excited to sleep.

Lindsey laughed, knowing what was coming. *And why's that?*

Thinking about you.

Was it possible to blush over a text? She knew better than to ask him specifically what he was thinking about. She'd confessed that she'd be flying in for game two tomorrow. *Are you counting down?* she wrote back.

Yep.

She hesitated over her reply, her pulse racing. Then she typed, *Me too.*

He typed back a smiling emoji, then wrote, *Are you going to conference me into your meeting with Dawson?*

Yeah, if you still want me to.

I do, he wrote.

This was a new aspect of life for Lindsey, having another person so closely involved with her life. It was nice, yet a little nerve-wracking as well since it only made her feel closer to Nelson, a guy who lived in another state. *Okay, we're meeting at 10 still.*

After texting Nelson, Lindsey got ready for the day, changing into a linen blouse to complement the warming weather in Pine Valley, along with gray slacks and gray high heels. She listened to the news as she pulled her hair into a twist, so when her phone rang, she jumped, not expecting a call so early.

She picked up her phone but didn't recognize the number. That wasn't unusual, especially since she'd changed her number, and she also had a notice out in the Pine Valley paper about her new law office.

"Hello, this is Lindsey Gerber," she answered.

No one answered, but she was pretty sure that someone was on the other end of the line. "Hello, can I help you?" she said, but nothing.

She muted the television to see if she could hear anything. But everything was quiet, although the prickling hairs on the back of her neck told her the caller was still on. She hung up the phone, then sent Dawson the number to see if he had it saved in his contacts.

She was mostly ready, so she watered her plants and turned them in front of the bay window. It was something she did every day—turning the plants each morning. Then she left her place, locked the door, and headed to the car she'd bought the week before. A used Acura. She hadn't needed a car in the city since public transportation was much easier and more convenient. But in Pine Valley, the winters were too cold to rely on walking or biking everywhere.

Besides, she liked to wear heels.

Once she reached the office, she returned some phone calls that had come into the main line, then met with a pair of potential clients at nine. They were a newly retired couple who had put together a will years ago, but with changes in their family, they wanted to revamp it.

The couple was pleasant and easy to talk to, and Lindsey wished all her meetings would go so smoothly.

By the time ten rolled around, Lindsey was ready for a break. She grabbed a water bottle from the small kitchenette Dawson had set up, then walked to his office. His door was half open, but he was on the phone.

Lindsey tapped on the door, and Dawson turned, then motioned for her to come inside. So she walked into his plush office and took a seat in one of the soft leather chairs.

Dawson laughed at something said by the person he was talking to, then he said, "I've got to jump into another meeting, so let's talk tomorrow." After he hung up, he swiveled fully to look at Lindsey. "I checked that number you sent over, and I don't have it as a contact in my phone."

"Oh, don't worry about it." Truth was, Lindsey had forgotten about it. "Nelson wants to be conferenced into the meeting so he can hear your report."

Dawson's brows arched, but a smile played on his face. "Is that so?"

"Yes, that's so," Lindsey said, having a hard time keeping back a smile. "He's being supportive, that's all."

Dawson tapped his pen to his mouth. "And you going to Vegas over the weekend was equally supportive?"

Lindsey laughed. "It was."

Dawson gave her a wink. "He's a decent guy; you could do worse."

"Oh, in that case, I appreciate your vote of support." Lindsey smirked, then set her phone on the desk, put it on speaker, and called Nelson.

He answered on the second ring, and after brief preliminaries, Dawson dove into his update and subsequent report. Lindsey had always been impressed with Dawson, but she was even more impressed with his thoroughness. He'd gotten much farther on the case than she'd realized.

Nelson asked a few questions, and Dawson had the answers.

"So they pay the asking settlement price," Nelson asked, "and the firm gets to keep their reputation in place, while Lindsey has to keep the details confidential?"

"Yes," Dawson said. "Lindsey will get a good sum of money to invest into her business or whatever she wants."

"How does Lindsey staying quiet prevent this kind of stuff happening again or ensure the firm learns its lesson?" Nelson pressed.

"Great questions," Dawson said. "I think Lindsey's the best one to answer."

"I don't have to keep the suit confidential," she said. "Only the terms of the settlement. The fact that there is a settlement is a big, red, guilty flag pointed at the firm. It's also meant to pinch them financially so that they'll hopefully adhere to their own sexual harassment policies."

"Is that what you want?" Nelson said.

"Yes." Lindsey didn't hesitate. She'd thought it through from all angles, long and hard. "Taking them to trial could take months, even longer."

"What about Paul?"

"Still on leave," Dawson said. "I doubt he'll be returning to the firm, though."

Dawson finished up his report, and when they hung up with Nelson, Dawson leaned back in his chair and gazed at Lindsey.

"What do you think?" he asked.

"I think you're amazing," Lindsey said. "I've never seen another lawyer be so thorough and pull things together so quickly."

Dawson shrugged. "I take care of my friends."

"Well, thank you," Lindsey said. "It means a lot to me, even though you'll be getting your cut."

Dawson chuckled. "You know, the more I talk to Nelson, the more I like him. I wasn't so sure at first."

"You mean when he almost punched you in the face?" Lindsey teased.

"Yeah, that wasn't pleasant," Dawson agreed with a smirk. "So you're going to try this long-distance relationship thing out for a while?"

Lindsey exhaled. "Yeah, I guess. It's not like he's going to quit hockey. And there aren't many pro teams in Pine Valley."

"And you?" Dawson asked. "You're committed here?"

"I am," Lindsey said. "But if things keep moving forward, I'll have a pretty serious decision to make."

Dawson raised a brow. "You think he might be the one?"

Lindsey looked away from Dawson's probing brown gaze for a second. He was being way too perceptive. But Dawson was a friend, one she implicitly trusted.

"I don't know," Lindsey said finally. "How's that for an answer? I mean, I'm sort of obsessed with him right now, but is that a good thing?"

"Well, he likes you, that's for sure," Dawson said. "He was asking all the right questions. And in his questions I could hear that he truly cares about you."

Lindsey could only nod because she couldn't speak for a moment. Finally, she said, "Yeah, but that's what scares me too." She blew out a breath. "Well, enough of that. Back to work."

Dawson nodded with a smile. "Let me know if you need anything," he said. "I'm leaving in about an hour for court, but I'll check my phone in between stuff."

"Great, thanks," Lindsey said. She returned to her office and called Nelson. She wanted to hear his voice again and have the conversation be between the two of them, with no middle man.

When she hung up, she was smiling. The office outside her door was absolutely silent, which meant that Dawson had left. She stood and adjusted the blinds against the bright sun. The sky was a brilliant blue, and the trees outside had burst into blossom.

Lindsey spent the next few hours in phone calls, sending emails, and texting Nelson once he was done with practice. She was surprised to see that it was nearly dark by the time she was finished with her to-do lists. Staying busy had been good, and she was looking forward to tomorrow, when she'd fly to Vegas and see Nelson play in game two.

She grabbed a to-go chicken sandwich on the way back to her place. It smelled heavenly, and she realized she'd worked straight through lunch without a thought to get something from the office kitchenette. She made her way to her condo, thinking of how she should probably start being friendlier to her neighbors if she was going to be in Pine Valley for a while. The small-town clientele wasn't keeping her busy night and day like her clientele in San Francisco had.

She smiled as she unlocked her front door. She could get used to this more relaxed place. Home before seven. Who would have thought?

The second she flipped on the lights, she knew something was different. Lindsey paused in the doorway, scanning the front room. Everything seemed to be in its place. The couch, the coffee table, the end table with a picture of her and her dad at her law school graduation. Her plants. They were still in the direction she'd turned them. Except for one.

She took a step back, then another, without shutting her door. There was no way she'd *not* turned the middle plant. Her routine was always the same, every day.

With trembling hands, she pulled out her cell phone and pressed SEND on Dawson's number. He might still be wrapped up in whatever court things he'd dealt with that day. "Please answer, please answer," she whispered into the phone as she headed to her car.

The dark parking lot was lit by the streetlamps, but that left plenty of shadows.

"Hey, Lindsey," Dawson's warm tone answered.

"Something's not right," she said, unable to hide the panic in her tone.

"Where are you?"

"My condo," she said, looking left, then right as she headed to her car.

"Leave and get in your car," Dawson said. "Lock all the doors."

"I am," she said, reaching for the door handle. She slipped into the car and locked the doors with a thudding click.

"Okay, I'm coming over," he said. "Hang up and call 911."

Lindsey released a shaky breath. "You don't think I'm overreacting?"

"If you're scared, that's reason enough," Dawson said. "Call them now."

"Okay," Lindsey said. "I'm calling." She hung up and dialed 911, hardly daring to believe she was doing this. When the dispatcher answered, Lindsey told her that someone had been in the apartment, although she'd locked the door.

"Does anyone have a spare key, ma'am?" the dispatcher asked after promising that a police officer was on his way.

"No," Lindsey said. "No one but me."

"Where are you now?" she asked.

"In my car, with the doors locked."

"That's great," the woman said. "Give me the information on your car, and I'll let the officer know where you are."

"My friend Dawson Harris is on his way over too."

"Noted," the dispatcher said.

Lindsey tried to answer the dispatcher's questions as calmly as possible, but her heart was pumping furiously. There had been no movement by her condo, and she had a clear view. She saw the cop car pull into the condo complex. He parked at the very end and then got out. The cop was tall with dark hair, and he made a beeline for her car.

She opened the door as he approached.

"I'm Officer Russo," he said. "Are you Lindsey Gerber?"

"Yes."

He nodded. "I'm calling for another officer, and then we'll go and check your place."

A truck pulled into the parking lot.

"That's Dawson Harris," she said.

Russo glanced over. "I know him. We'll get this figured out, ma'am. Don't worry."

Twenty

Nelson had just walked into his place, a sack of takeout food in hand, when his phone rang. He looked at the incoming call. *Dawson Harris.* The last person Nelson expected a call from.

"Hello?"

"Nelson? I'm calling to say that Lindsey is fine."

Now Nelson was worried. "What's going on?"

"Lindsey had a break-in tonight at her condo," Dawson said. "She wasn't touched or hurt or anything, and the cops got the intruder. She's at the police station right now, giving a report, and then she'll be staying at my place tonight, although her condo has now been cleared—"

"Whoa, whoa," Nelson said, setting his sack of food on the kitchen table and pacing the room. "There was an intruder at her place? Was he there to steal something? Or was he targeting Lindsey?"

Dawson was silent for a moment.

"Harris!"

"I'm not supposed to say anything, but it was Paul Locker."

Nelson stopped pacing as a cold shudder passed through him. "What the hell?"

"He's in custody now, and they're throwing everything at him," Dawson said. "I'm making sure of it. He won't be bothering Lindsey again."

"*How* are you making sure of it?"

Dawson exhaled. "The investigation is ongoing, and the details aren't public, so if I tell you, you can't say anything to anyone."

"Tell me," Nelson said, gripping the top of one of the kitchen chairs. In truth, he wanted to punch a wall, but that might come later.

"Paul Locker entered her apartment about six tonight," Dawson said. "He told the cops he was looking for paperwork or some sort of evidence that she was setting him up to get him fired. But the cops didn't find anything disturbed that would indicate he was telling the truth. They found him . . . in her bathtub with the curtain closed. Hiding."

Nelson had no response, because his mind had already gone to the worst-case scenario.

"He claims he'd gone in there because he panicked when he heard the door open to the apartment."

Nelson exhaled. "Do you think he panicked?"

"No," Dawson said. "I think he was there to harm her."

Nelson closed his eyes. He felt the same away, and he wanted to throw up. "Damn. What if she'd gone into the condo? What if—"

"Believe me, I've been over and over this too," Dawson said. "Bottom line is that Paul Locker is in the county jail, no bail set. And I'm going to make sure he won't be getting out anytime soon."

Nelson began to pace his kitchen again. "How's Lindsey?" he asked.

"Holding it together," Dawson said. "She's seen plenty of desperation in her line of work."

"This is *personal*, though," Nelson said. "Text me your address. I might be able to get there tonight."

"Don't you have a game—?"

"Screw the game," Nelson said. "Send me your address, but don't say anything to Lindsey. I don't want her to worry about one more thing."

When Nelson hung up with Dawson, he stood in the middle of his kitchen for a full minute, staring at the far wall. He'd never felt so helpless in his life. Lindsey could have been assaulted tonight, or worse. Much worse. And he was sitting in Vegas worrying about a little swelling in his pansy knee.

He called his teammate Blaine. When Blaine answered, Nelson said, "I need a really big favor, and I need it now."

An hour later, Nelson was on a private jet heading out of Vegas. Blaine had called his former college friend Cole Hunter, who was now a pro baseball player but happened to be wealthy beyond the average pro-baseball paycheck. Cole Hunter owned his own private jet and belonged to a club where he had other private jets at his disposal. Nelson was now on one of those jets.

The flight was quick, yet not quick enough. Nelson hated any delay. And when the plane landed at the closest regional airstrip to Pine Valley, a car was waiting to take him wherever he needed. Nelson sent Dawson a quick text that he was in Pine Valley and would be at his place soon.

"Thank you, Cole Hunter," Nelson murmured as he slid into the back seat and gave the driver Dawson's address.

Blaine had sent over Cole Hunter's contact info, and as the luxury car headed into Pine Valley, Nelson sent a text to Cole. Never mind that it was nearly midnight.

I can't thank you enough for arranging a charter for me tonight. —Tyler Nelson

The reply came seconds later. Apparently Cole Hunter was a night owl. *When Blaine told me it was to help out your girlfriend, I had no problem. Ladies always come first.*

About the only thing that Nelson knew about Cole was that he'd been part of the famous Belltown Six Pack of college baseball players who all got called up to the major leagues the same year. Also that he was from Texas and now played centerfield for the Los Angeles Sea Rays.

If you want premium tickets to the Stanley Cup, I'm your guy, Nelson wrote.

Thanks, man. I'm in season right now, so it would depend on a few factors. But I wish y'all good luck.

Definitely a Texan.

The dots on the text app jumped again. Cole was still texting. *The jet will wait for twenty-four hours to take you back to Vegas. If you need longer, then shoot me a text.*

This Nelson wasn't expecting. He'd fully prepared to call Coach and tell him to put Ben in for game two. *Thanks, I'll let you know.*

No problem, Cole wrote. *Give your darlin' my best.*

Nelson smiled at the text. Cole's Texan endearment had pretty much nailed how Nelson felt about Lindsey.

He didn't know what to expect when he reached Dawson Harris's place, but the lights were on inside his condo.

Did that mean Lindsey was awake too?

Nelson thanked the driver, who gave him his cell number so that Nelson could call for a return ride to the airstrip. Then he headed to Dawson's front door and knocked softly.

Dawson opened the door almost immediately. Nelson had never seen the guy dressed down, but now Dawson wore a simple T-shirt and athletic shorts. He was also barefoot, and there were tired lines around his eyes. So the guy could be stressed and wasn't all suave all the time.

"I didn't tell her you were coming," Dawson said in a quiet voice. "She's in the back bedroom at the end of the hall. Just knock and announce yourself before going in."

Nelson nodded. "How's she doing?"

"She says she's fine, but she's not fooling me." Dawson put a hand on Nelson's shoulder, surprising him. "I'm glad you're here."

Nelson didn't know if that made him feel better or worse. How upset was Lindsey? He couldn't imagine what she'd gone through, and he still felt sick about how close of a call it was. Nelson headed down the hallway to the final door. Light glowed beneath the door, but he couldn't hear anything.

He knocked, then said, "Lindsey, it's me, Nelson."

He heard a clink, then seconds later the door opened.

Lindsey stared at him with wide eyes. Her dark hair tumbled about her shoulders, and she wore no makeup, but that only made her look more beautiful and vulnerable. "What are you doing here?" she whispered, opening the door wider.

Nelson stepped into the room. "Dawson told me what happened, so here I am."

Lindsey threw her arms about his neck, and he pulled her close.

"I still don't get it," she said in a trembling voice. "How did you get here?"

"A friend hooked me up with his jet." Nelson breathed in her warmth. She was okay. She was here, safe. But he hated that he hadn't been around when it happened. Or that he couldn't have found a way to stop it in the first place.

Lindsey was still clinging to him, and Nelson used his foot to nudge the door shut. He ran his hands up and down her back. "Are you okay?"

"Much better now," she said, then she drew away to look at him, although she kept her arms looped about his neck. "I can't believe you're here."

Nelson lifted a hand and smoothed the hair from her face. "Anything for you, babe."

Her eyes filled with tears, and the impact went straight to his gut.

"Thank you," she whispered, blinking. "Did you have to miss practice?"

"No, it's the middle of the night," he said.

The edges of her mouth lifted.

"That's better," he said, running his fingers along her cheek. "Tell me what happened."

She swallowed, then nodded. "You know it was Paul, right?"

"Yeah, Dawson told me." He tried to keep the steely edge out of his voice. She didn't need his anger right now. She needed to be able to tell her story.

Lindsey stepped back from him and grasped his hand. She led him to the loveseat on the other side of the bed. They sat down, and Lindsey leaned against him, then Nelson wrapped his arms about her.

"When I got home earlier tonight," she said, "I opened the door, and it was weird, but I felt something was different."

Nelson nodded. "Your instincts warned you."

"I couldn't figure it out at first, but then I noticed one of my plants by the bay window had been turned."

Goose bumps raced along Nelson's skin. "That was observant."

"That's what Officer Russo said, you know, the cop who arrived first," she continued. Then she told him about the rest, about the cops finding Paul hiding in the shower, and how she'd watched him being led in handcuffs to the police car.

Her tone was matter-of-fact, but Nelson heard the tremor in her voice. Without saying it, they both knew that had Lindsey gone inside her condo, the outcome could have been much worse.

Nelson rubbed her arm and kissed the top of her head. "Dawson said that he'll be put away for a long time. And if that doesn't happen, I'll come up with something else that might be a bit illegal."

Lindsey released a soft laugh. Nelson hadn't meant to be funny; in fact, he was dead serious. But hearing Lindsey relax was better than he could have hoped.

She didn't say anything for a long moment, and by the way she was fully leaning against him, he wondered if she'd fallen asleep.

But a few moments later, she said, "Thanks for coming, Nelson. You're making it really hard not to fall in love with you."

Nelson didn't move, didn't answer. He was stunned. Had she just said . . . Her breathing evened out and deepened.

He leaned forward ever so carefully and snagged the bedspread from the bed. Then he draped it over the both of them. With Lindsey's head on his shoulder and her arms wrapped about his torso, he leaned his head back and closed his eyes.

He didn't know if he'd be able to sleep like this, and he should probably transfer Lindsey to the bed, then find a longer couch somewhere. But the adrenaline of the night was wearing off, and Nelson was reluctant to disturb her. So he stayed put, and eventually, his body decided it didn't matter where he slept.

Twenty-one

The first thing Lindsey heard when she woke up was someone breathing.

Before she opened her eyes, she remembered that Nelson had shown up unexpectedly last night. And he hadn't left.

His chest and torso were warm, and even though his muscles were sturdy, he was surprisingly comfortable to sleep on. She guessed the time to be late morning, which meant . . .

"Nelson," she said, pulling away from him.

He blinked those beautiful gray eyes open.

"Don't you have practice or something?"

His gaze searched hers, and he didn't say anything for a moment. "I'm not going." His voice was still raspy with sleep, which made her feel a twinge of guilt.

Lindsey moved his arm that was around her. "What do you mean? Your game is tonight. Don't you have team stuff?"

Nelson sat up more fully and stifled a yawn. Then he

drew her back into his arms, which felt pretty great, but she didn't think he should be delaying so much.

"Do you always wake up hyper?" he rasped.

"Nelson, I'm serious, you need to go."

His hold only tightened about her. "Mmm." He wasn't moving, wasn't releasing her.

"Nelson..."

He moved his hand up her back, then over her shoulder, and finally behind her neck, where his fingers tangled in her hair. Being touched by him was like heaven, but she couldn't give into this. There was a good chance he'd already missed whatever morning workout his coach made the team do.

"I'm officially kicking you out, Nelson," she said.

He chuckled, then he shifted and kissed her.

Well, good morning. His sleepy kiss was pretty dang sexy, and Lindsey almost forgot why Nelson had come to Pine Valley in the middle of the night in the first place.

When he lifted his head, he was smiling.

"You're trying to distract me," she said.

"Is it working?" he said, then he kissed her again.

Oh, it's working, her heart sang. She slid her arms around his neck and allowed herself to live in another existence that contained only this man and his body and his mouth. She didn't even know if Dawson was still in the condo, and she really didn't care.

"You being quiet in the morning is much better," Nelson said.

Lindsey slapped his shoulder and laughed. "You did not just say that."

Nelson gazed at her, his gray eyes full of... desire. The kind that made her breathless.

"How are you feeling?" he asked.

Of course he'd ask that. Here he was, probably pissing off his whole team, but he wanted to know how she was feeling.

"I'm okay," she said, and it was the truth. Where Nelson was concerned, she was better than okay, but the fact that Paul Locker had shown up at her condo last night was something that would take a while to get over. "And I'd be better if I knew you were on your way back to Vegas."

"I'll go back if you come with me," he said. "You were flying out this afternoon, anyway, right?"

"Right."

The edges of his mouth curved.

"Oh, all right, I'll come, but only because it's a private jet."

He chuckled, then kissed her jaw, her neck, and lower.

Lindsey truly didn't mind, but Dawson could very well still be in the condo. "Nelson," she said, disentangling herself from his grasp. "I need to get my stuff at my apartment and shower and stuff. Can you . . . come with me?"

He didn't hesitate. "Of course."

"Thanks," she said, and when he stood, she wrapped her arms about his torso and held on for a few moments.

He obliged her with another embrace that lasted far too long to be anything but innocent.

"Thanks for coming last night," she said against his chest. "I hope you don't get in trouble."

"I'm not worried," his voice rumbled above her. "If Coach decides to sit me, then he'll be putting the entire game at risk."

She smiled, although he couldn't see it. "True."

Two hours later, they'd landed in Vegas, and they were on their way to his condo so that he could get ready for the pre-game meeting and warm-up. In the Uber, Nelson held her hand, and Lindsey felt like she'd lived five lifetimes since her last, carefree visit to Vegas.

"My sister is coming to the game too," he said. "And

she'll be crashing at my place, so you're welcome to stay of course. My sister is good at keeping me in line."

"Hmm, maybe I will then," Lindsey said. It might be good to get to know his sister better, because it would give her even more insight into this amazing man. Maybe Lindsey would finally crack some of his flaws. "But where will you sleep?"

"Well, if you won't let me share your bed, then I guess I'll take the couch." He winked.

"I can't make you stay on the couch in your own place," she said.

He leaned over and whispered in her ear. "Then we'll share my bed, and I promise I won't kick you."

"Funny."

He squeezed her hand. "The couch will feel like heaven compared to that tiny loveseat at Dawson's."

"Sorry about that," she said.

Nelson kissed her cheek. "It was the best night's sleep that I've ever had."

She swatted his chest, but he caught her hand and held it there. He kissed her again, this time just below her jaw.

Lindsey wanted to pull him close and kiss him for real, but she didn't really want to kiss in the back of an Uber.

"I think you'll enjoy the couch after all," she said.

Nelson chuckled, and Lindsey smiled. The more she was with Nelson, the more she forgot about Paul Locker. Dawson said he was going to figure out how Paul had tracked her down, but in the end, did it matter? He'd shown up, and who knew what his real plans were? Right now, Lindsey was grateful to be in another state, away from Paul, even if he was in jail.

When the Uber stopped at Nelson's condo complex, he grabbed her carry-on suitcase from the trunk of the car, then thanked the driver.

They went into his condo, and the first thing that Lindsey smelled was the scent of old food. A fast-food sack was on the kitchen table.

Nelson crossed to it immediately. "Forgot I'd left this here last night," he said. "I'll just go and dump it in the trash outside. You can open a window if you want."

When he was gone, Lindsey opened the windows in the living room, then settled onto the couch. Even though she'd done nothing today, she felt tired. Dawson said he'd handle any walk-ins at the office, and she'd already emailed others to reschedule the morning meetings she'd had that day.

Nelson came back into the condo. "Sorry about that."

"You must have left in a hurry," she said, knowing it was so.

"Yeah," he said. "Once Dawson called, my mind was on only one track."

Those gray eyes of his were gazing at her in a way that made a lump form in her throat.

"So, uh," he said, rubbing a hand over his hair. "I'm going to shower, and then I need to take off. Help yourself to whatever you need. Becca should be here in a couple of hours, and you two can ride over to the arena together."

"Okay," Lindsey said. While he was in the shower, she picked up an album on the side table next to the couch. It looked like it was full of pictures from the Falcons. Most of them were from games, but there were some from gala events and what looked to be fundraisers. Lindsey stopped on a particular picture where Nelson had his arm slung over the shoulders of a young woman.

"That's my sister." Nelson's voice cut into Lindsey's thoughts. She hadn't even heard him come down the hallway.

She looked over at him and wished she hadn't. He was obviously fresh from the shower, and well, he wasn't wearing a shirt. He wore athletic shorts and had a towel around his neck. She'd hugged him plenty and had imagined more than once what his chest and torso looked like, but her imagination hadn't done Tyler Nelson justice.

"Are you okay?" Nelson asked.

She was literally staring. "Uh, yes," she said, trying to focus on something that wasn't his magnificent body. But there seemed to be nowhere else to look. "Did you forget a shirt?"

He blinked, then he grinned. "I came out to get some water. Should I go put on my shirt before doing so?"

She swallowed. Him standing there, leaning against the corner of the wall, his torso practically begging to be touched, wasn't making her resolve any easier. "Well, I guess it's your place, so you can decide."

He nodded and turned from her, then headed into the kitchen.

Oh boy. Seeing his bare back was doing even crazier things to her insides. *Look at the album, Lindsey.* She had to drag her gaze from the man in the kitchen guzzling down a cold water bottle and look at the album in her lap. She only saw a blur of pictures that might have faces and other things in them, but she wasn't sure.

"Do you want a drink?" Nelson asked from the kitchen.

"No, I'm okay," she had to choke out.

Nelson headed back down the hall, chuckling to himself.

Lindsey used the photo album to fan herself. How soon did he say his sister was arriving? A handful of minutes later, Nelson was back, with a shirt on.

He crossed to her. "Are you okay here by yourself?"

"Of course," she said. "Unless you have evil lawyers around."

"Not that I know of." His tone was teasing, but his gaze

was sober. He leaned down and set his hands on either side of the couch behind her head. "Bye."

"Bye," she said.

He kissed her. It was a brief kiss, but it still stirred up the butterflies in her stomach. His freshly showered scent was divine.

"See you soon," he said.

"See you," she repeated. "Good luck at your game. I'll be cheering for you."

He smiled and pushed up from the couch. He picked up the duffle bag next to the door, then opened the door.

She watched him leave, and when he shut and locked the door, she sagged against the couch. Tyler Nelson had her heart. There was no denying it.

Twenty-two

The Florida Ducks had a few moves up their sleeves that Nelson hadn't seen on any of their game film. Nelson knew that his absolute focus would be paramount and that he'd just have to forget that Lindsey and his sister were sitting next to each other in the stands.

Minky was on fire, though, and he scored in the first eight minutes of the first period. The Ducks retaliated with a point of their own, sending Nelson into a spiral of adrenaline. He was determined to not let another puck through. By the beginning of the second period, the score was one to one. Unacceptable.

Nelson was barely aware of the screaming crowd. He had a job to focus on. As the Ducks broke the Falcons' line of defense over and over, Nelson deflected goal shots one after the other. Game one hadn't been nearly as intense, and it was obvious that the Ducks' forwards had spent plenty of time analyzing Nelson's weaknesses. Because they were aiming for each one.

Blaine scored, pretty much saving the team and their entire season. And by the time the final buzzer sounded in the third period, Nelson was completely exhausted. He was also pissed at the halfbacks and fullbacks, who'd been more than lax. He moved off the ice with the rest of his team but didn't say a word. Not even when Minky clapped him on the back and said, "Nice job, man. You saved us again."

Nelson just shook his head. In the locker room, he nodded at Blaine, then went straight to the trainer after his shower. Ricky iced down Nelson's knee and asked a couple of questions, but when he realized Nelson wasn't much for talking, Ricky worked in silence.

Because of the ice-down, Nelson was the last one out of the locker room. Coach had even left, probably to do more interviews with the media. Nelson purposely headed down the corridor that would lead him away from fans and signing opportunities. When he reached the parking lot, he saw his sister with Lindsey, standing near his truck. His sister had done the right thing then, not waiting for him by a portal.

"Nice game, Ty," Becca said with a wide smile on her face. She'd bleached her hair again, making it about five shades lighter than his dirty blond. And her blue-gray eyes that were so much like his were focused on him like an arrow. Despite her smile, she recognized his mood.

"Thanks, sis," he said, his answer short and curt.

Becca hugged him, and he held her tightly for a moment. It was good to see her, but his anger about the game still hadn't settled down. "Thanks for coming," he tried again, hopefully keeping the edge out of his voice.

Then Becca released him and stepped back.

Lindsey was watching him, a frown between her brows.

"Sorry I'm so pissy," he said, stepping to Lindsey. He kissed her on the cheek, keeping it brief. "Rough game."

Becca nodded. "I know. That's why we ordered your favorite barbeque to pick up on the way to your place."

Nelson gave his sister a smile, although he didn't feel like smiling. "Thanks, sis."

Becca linked arms with Lindsey. "No problem. It was Lindsey's idea, actually. Said you're always starving after the games."

Nelson linked his fingers with Lindsey's and squeezed. He should probably go running or something, blow off the steam that had been building for the last ninety minutes of hockey.

Once they had picked up the food and made it back to his condo, Nelson was pretty sure his sister had become best friends with Lindsey. The two women had chattered nonstop in the truck, and Lindsey had laughed at all the stories that Becca had shared, some about their childhood.

Nelson didn't mind, not at all, but he sort of wished he could go crash and start over tomorrow. Talking to Coach about the team wouldn't help, not this late in the season. Everyone was stressed, and everyone was already doing their thing. No matter how many times Nelson called out direction to the fullbacks, they'd ignored him. He wondered if it had something to do with his three-week absence. Had they all bonded with Ben that much?

Had they not seen Ben's blatant mistakes, things that no professional goaltender should be doing?

"Hello, Tyler?" his sister's voice cut into his thoughts.

He looked over at his sister. Both women had finished eating, and he had hardly touched the food he'd piled onto his plate.

"Not hungry after all?" Becca asked.

"I am . . . Sorry. The game's still in my head."

"No worries, bro," she said, standing, then patting his

shoulder. "I'm beat, and I have an early flight. So I'm going to read a little, then go to sleep."

"What time do you need a ride to the airport?" he asked.

"Oh, I've scheduled a Lyft," she said. "I'm not going to make even my brother drive me at four thirty in the morning."

"I can take you, Becca," he said. "It's fine."

"No, you sleep," she said. "You need to be rested for your travel to Florida and your next game against the Quacks."

Normally Nelson would have laughed, but he barely forced out a smile. "Okay, but seriously, if you change your mind, just wake me up. I'll be on the couch."

Becca's eyebrows rose, and she looked from him to Lindsey. "Okay then. Goodnight. And great to meet you, Lindsey."

Lindsey stood and hugged Becca, then Becca headed down the hall to the guest bedroom.

After the bedroom door clicked shut, Nelson met Lindsey's gaze. "Sorry about all this," he said. "I'm being a terrible host."

Lindsey shrugged. "Don't worry about me. I'm fine. Becca's been great."

"Good." He hesitated. "Would you mind if I went for a run? I've got to get some things worked out in my head."

Worry flickered in Lindsey's eyes, but she nodded. "Sure. You go, I'll clean up here."

"Thanks, babe," he said.

He went into his bedroom and tugged on his running shoes, then grabbed a couple of things that he'd need when he returned and slept on the couch. He dumped them on the couch on his way out. Lindsey had the kitchen-sink water running when he left.

Nelson walked out of the parking lot and started to jog down the neighborhood road. He'd done everything but jog since his injury, yet he wasn't going to let a little achiness stop him. He had a lot to think about, and exercising alone was the best way he knew how to do it.

His thoughts first went to Lindsey, and even though he knew he was in season, he still didn't like the long-distance thing. When she'd told him last night that she was falling in love with him, even though he was pretty sure she didn't remember saying it, those words had cut straight into his soul. Because he knew he was feeling the same way.

And seeing her with Becca only solidified it. Becca was his only family, and if she liked Lindsey, that pretty much sealed the deal.

Nelson turned a corner and upped his pace now that he was warmed up. He didn't like that his team felt different. Sure, he was still close to Minky, and Blaine had done him a huge favor by hooking him up with Cole Hunter's private-jet service, but there was no real friendship with the other guys. Coach looked at Nelson like a commodity—which he was, and which he wasn't going to argue with—but when Nelson saw things that were broken on the team, it was like he was talking to a wall if he brought it up to Coach.

He'd been in this same situation during one club season in high school. The team he'd been on had established cliques, or a good ole boys club, when Nelson came on. Nelson hadn't been there to make friends in the first place, but he'd been aware of the times that the teammates got together after games or practices. He'd never been invited. And he truly hadn't cared, as long as the team was in sync during games.

Nothing was in sync right now, not in his professional life or his personal life.

Lindsey could have been seriously hurt by a damn intruder the night before, and even though Paul Locker was behind bars, Nelson was frustrated that he lived hundreds of miles away from the woman he loved and should be protecting.

Yeah, he loved her.

And he didn't know what to do about it.

By the time Nelson returned to the condo, everything was quiet. A single light had been left on in the living room, but there were no lights coming from either of the bedroom doors. No wonder, since it was after one in the morning. Nelson had run until he almost couldn't walk anymore, but he'd figured a few things out. And if he still felt the same way in the morning, then he was going to begin putting his plan into action.

No one would know until it was a done deal. Not even Lindsey.

Nelson showered, then changed into the clothes he'd dumped on the couch. He hoped his mind would slow down enough that he could get some sleep. He planned to take his team to the Stanley Cup, win the whole thing, then . . .

It felt like he'd just fallen asleep when he sensed someone walking into the living room. It took him a second to remember why he was on the couch in the first place. When he opened his eyes, he saw Becca opening the front door.

"You're out of here?" Nelson asked, sitting up on the couch.

"Yeah," Becca whispered. "Sorry to wake you."

Nelson rose and crossed the room to hug her goodbye. "You know I can drive you to the airport."

She squeezed him and patted his back. "I know, but the car's already waiting outside. Thanks, though. You're a good brother."

Nelson drew away. "Have a safe trip."

Becca smiled. "I will. And take care of that girlfriend of yours. You're a lucky guy."

All for You

"You like her?" Nelson said, although he knew the answer.

"She's amazing, like you said," Becca said. "If you screw things up with her, you'll have me to answer to."

Nelson chuckled. "Duly noted."

Becca gave him another quick hug and hurried out the door. Nelson shut it quietly, then turned the deadbolt. He returned to the couch. His mind was fully awake now, and he was pretty sure he was done sleeping, even though he'd only gotten at most three hours of sleep. But he didn't want to move around the condo, since it would probably wake up Lindsey.

So he settled back onto the couch, propping his hands behind his head, and watched the changing shadows on the ceiling as the early dawn approached. Nothing he'd decided last night felt off, and he was determined to go forward with his plans.

"Nelson?" The whisper brought him out of his thoughts, and he looked over to see Lindsey. She was wearing a long T-shirt of some sort.

"Sorry, did we wake you?" he said. "I tried to be quiet."

"I've been awake for a while," she said. "Is Becca gone?"

"Yeah, she left a few minutes ago." He narrowed his eyes. "Is that my shirt?"

She looked down at what she was wearing. "Oh, I forgot my PJs. I hope you don't mind."

"Come over here, and I'll let you know if I mind." He scooted over on the couch, turning on his side, and Lindsey sat next to him. "Closer," he said.

She lay down alongside him, and facing him, she nestled against the length of his body.

He drew her close and kissed her temple. "You smell good."

She smiled and closed her eyes, wrapping her arms about

his torso. He was pretty sure she could feel the racing thump of his heart.

"How was your run last night?" she asked.

"Long, but good," he said. "Thanks for putting up with me."

Her laugh was soft, like a caress.

"Did you sleep?" he whispered.

"Not really," she said. "I kept waking up, thinking of you out here, on the couch."

"It's pretty comfortable, don't you think?"

She laughed again, and he smiled.

"How are you doing?" he asked, knowing that the question wasn't just a casual one.

"Good right now," she said. "So when's that fifth game?"

"Well, if we need a fifth game, it will be next Sunday in Vegas."

"Okay, I'll come."

Warmth buzzed through him. "I'd love that. And I promise not to be a head case."

She ran her hand up his arm. "You're not a head case, Nelson. You're one of the best goaltenders in the league, and you deserve teammates who are as dedicated as you."

"Have you been talking to Becca?"

"Yes." She lifted up on her elbow. "I like her a lot."

He gazed into her eyes, a darker color in the dimness. "And what about me?" he whispered. "Do you like *me*?"

The edges of her lips curved. "Very much." She closed the distance between them and kissed him lightly on the lips.

He wanted more, much more, yet there was something significant at this moment. He didn't know what it was, but he didn't want to ruin it. He smoothed some of her hair from her face, then let his fingers linger on her neck. "I like you very much too," he said.

Lindsey smiled, then moved to lay her head against his shoulder.

"I can have Ben take my place for the next game if you want me to go back to Pine Valley with you," he said. "You know, to make sure you're okay in your condo."

"I'll be fine, I promise," she said. "Besides, I'm not going to come between you and your team. That's your job, your commitment. And I can't go to Florida, because I have to get my business producing."

"We sure have a lot of commitments between the two of us," he said. Commitments that were keeping them apart.

Lindsey released a soft sigh but didn't respond.

Minutes passed, and she gradually relaxed more, until her breathing evened out and she fell asleep once again in his arms.

This was nice, Nelson decided. He wouldn't be sleeping, but he was more than happy to be her sleeping place. He wouldn't mind more of this. Much more.

Twenty-three

Lindsey stepped off the plane, back in Vegas two weeks later for game five of the Stanley Cup. She couldn't believe Nelson's team had made it this far. She was so proud of him, and despite all the dissension that was only getting worse among his teammates, Nelson had kept his focus with his usual grit.

Becca had informed Lindsey about the underbelly of the world of pro sports, giving her quite an education. Speaking of Becca, she was waving wildly at Lindsey from the baggage-claim area. They'd coordinated their flights so that they could share a car and head over to the game together.

Nelson would already be at the arena, so Lindsey wouldn't be able to see him until after game five. Which could very well be the final game, since the Falcons had won three and the Boston Devils had won once.

Lindsey hurried to Becca and hugged the woman.

"It's so good to see you!" Becca said, her perfect white

teeth flashing as she grinned. "I don't know how you wear those heels all the time."

Lindsey laughed. "I'm used to them, I guess. They didn't really stand out in San Francisco, but in Pine Valley . . . well, not many women wear heels."

Becca smirked. "And I think my brother likes them."

Lindsey gave a noncommittal shrug. In truth, things were getting more and more serious with Nelson. Whether they were spending brief amounts of time together when she came to Vegas for his games or they were on the phone, talking or texting, a shift had happened since that night Lindsey had first met Becca.

Lindsey's relationship with Nelson had gone from fun and lighthearted to more intense, more real. More everything.

"So, you checked your luggage?" Lindsey asked.

"Yeah, I brought stuff to decorate Tyler's place," Becca said. "So they'd better win tonight. If not, then the decorations will have to stick around a while."

Lindsey laughed. "Sounds great to me. Even if they don't win the Cup, it's amazing they've gotten this far."

"Don't let Tyler hear you say that," Becca said with a grimace. "*Almost* isn't good enough for these alphas."

"Well, hopefully this game will be a win, so I won't have to."

Becca snorted. "True. And that's why I like you. You're not afraid to state your opinion."

"I'm sort of required to," Lindsey said. "For my job, that is."

"Oh, there's my bag," Becca said, then she moved to the conveyor belt and pulled off a dark-green suitcase. "First stop, Tyler's place."

Lindsey and Becca spent the next hour decorating Nelson's condo, from hanging banners and streamers to blowing up balloons. "This looks like Mardi Gras," Lindsey pronounced when they were done.

Becca laughed. "Tyler's gonna hate it, which will make it even better. Did you know he won't even allow leftovers in his fridge?"

"Yeah," Lindsey said. "We should fill up his fridge too. If only to mess with him."

"Ooh," Becca said. "I like the way you think." She checked her cell. "We don't have to be at the game for two hours, so let's go grocery shopping."

The two women were in their arena seats about twenty minutes before start time. Because of their extra errands, they'd been dropped off by the Lyft later than they'd planned. But it had been worth it. Nelson's fridge was now stocked with food and some gag items.

Lindsey stood with the crowd for the national anthem, placing her hand over her heart. Her pulse raced, and she felt the tension and anticipation radiating from every single person in the arena, no matter who they were here to support.

Then the light dimmed and the music boomed as the Jumbotron overhead blared to life with cameo appearances from the Falcon players, including Nelson. Then the arena went dead quiet as a man dressed in all leather skated to the center of the ice and a single spotlight followed him. He came to a stop, then held out his gloved hand. A falcon dove straight from the arena ceiling, flying straight for the man's arm.

The spectators gasped as they watched the falcon land on the man's arm. Then the man gave another command, and the falcon flew straight toward the audience, then made a last-minute turn and circled the arena.

After the bird show, the announcer walked out onto the ice to the cheering crowd. He announced the starting lineup, and Lindsey cheered along with Becca. And when Nelson's name was announced, she cheered again.

The game started, and some of the fans remained standing, since the Falcons were making a hard drive to their opponents' side. When Minky scored, the arena went wild. Then, a few minutes later, another Falcons forward scored.

Two to zero. That was good, really good, Lindsey thought. But she was having trouble catching a full breath as she watched the intense, violent game, all in the pursuit of possessing a three-inch puck.

Lindsey could breathe a little better going into the second period. She watched Nelson on the bench with his teammates during the intermission. He unlaced his skates and sat on the end of the bench, not talking to anyone after the coach made some sort of speech.

"He must really be in the zone," Lindsey said to Becca.

"He always is," she said. "Even as a kid. His teammates learn pretty quick not to talk to him until after the game, and even then, it might be risky."

Yeah, Lindsey had been a witness to at least one night like that. She wished she could be around Nelson more, there for him more, and not bouncing back and forth. Even after the Stanley Cup championship, he said that everyone got a couple of weeks off, then it was back to conditioning.

And then what would their relationship look like? Random weekends back and forth? Even though Lindsey hadn't told Nelson how serious her feelings had become for him, she was pretty sure he'd guessed. Dawson had guessed too.

That morning, he'd come into her office as she was finishing up a phone call. When she'd hung up, he'd helped himself to the chair across from her desk. "Tell Nelson good luck tonight."

"Thanks, I will." Lindsey was grateful for Dawson's friendship and his support, and most especially for him representing her case, both against her former firm and now against Paul Locker.

"You know, Lindsey, when you first signed the one-year lease, I thought it was a good idea."

Lindsey frowned. "What do you mean? Have you changed your mind?"

"No." Dawson leaned forward, his brown eyes focused on her. "But I think you have."

For a moment, Lindsey didn't say anything. Then she exhaled. "I have been thinking about it, but I'm still unsure."

"Well, if it helps, I won't hold you to the lease terms," Dawson said. "I'm sure I'll be able to find someone to rent the office to. Maybe a realtor or something."

His words had sent a flood of nerves and new possibilities through her. She'd thanked him, and she'd been thinking of what Nelson's reaction would be if she told him she was willing to relocate to Vegas. Would he be happy? Or would he think their relationship was moving too fast, in a direction he wasn't ready for or interested in?

The buzzer rang, and third period was underway. Nelson was back on the ice, defending his goal. Lindsey loved watching him in action. She loved seeing him succeed in what he loved. She loved talking to him. She loved how protective he was of her, how supportive. She loved his texts, his phone calls, the way he hugged her. Teased her. Kissed her. She loved him. And suddenly her decision to relocate seemed very easy.

Happiness bubbled through her as she watched the action on the ice. Being with Nelson had become her whole world. She didn't know how it had happened, but it had.

One of the Ducks' players skated past the final Falcons' defense and shot. Nelson deflected the puck, and the arena cheered, but in the next instant, the Ducks regained control and shot again.

The puck slid into the very corner of the goal.

The arena erupted with both cheers and groans.

Ducks: one. Falcons: two.

Everything heated up then. The players. The fans. The tension in the arena.

Becca grabbed Lindsey's hand, and she hung on as they watched the game clock count down while the players below tried to make history. Lindsey felt both sick and exhilarated at the same time. Five minutes. Four minutes. Three minutes.

Another shot on Nelson. He deflected it, and the crowd roared.

Linsey was shouting too, without even making sense. She just felt like she had to shout something.

Two minutes. One.

The buzzer rang, and the arena erupted in celebration.

Lindsey stared in stunned silence, then started screaming. "They won!"

Becca was jumping up and down next to her, screaming as well. The two women hugged fiercely, then Becca hugged the woman on her other side.

Lindsey didn't know if she was laughing or crying, but tears ran down her face. The Falcons made a circuit around the ice, holding up their hockey sticks in triumph as the crowd continued to cheer and celebrate.

"Oh my gosh, they really won," Lindsey said, covering her mouth and blinking back tears. Her entire body was trembling.

The announcer was back on the ice, talking about the prestige of the Stanley Cup, and then he announced that Tyler Nelson was the season's MVP.

Lindsey and Becca cheered and watched as Nelson went to accept the trophy for the team. He lifted up the giant silver cup and skated with it around the rink, holding it above his head. The arena cheered as everyone filmed the moment with their phones. Next, Minky took over and skated another circuit.

Lindsey continued to wipe tears as she watched the teammates each take a turn. The crowd didn't seem to be going anywhere, and after all the announcing was over, Lindsey and Becca had to weave through people to make it down the bleachers to the bench.

Nelson had taken off his helmet, face mask, and outer goalie pads by the time they got through the throng of people. Becca reached him first and threw her arms about his neck. "Congratulations, bro. I knew you could pull it off!"

Nelson grinned as he hugged her tight, then he looked over at Lindsey.

She almost forgot to breathe. Nelson was a beautiful specimen in his victory. His hair was mussed from his helmet, and perspiration glistened on his face, but the joy in his eyes was unforgettable.

He released Becca, and Lindsey moved forward next. He scooped her into a bear hug, lifting her from the ground.

"That was amazing, Nelson," she said against his ear, holding onto him as if she wasn't planning on letting him go anytime soon.

"Thanks, babe," he said.

People jostled against them as they tried to reach players, and the media wasn't far away, interviewing others. But Nelson didn't seem to notice. He set her back on her feet, but instead of letting her go, he cradled her face with his hands and kissed her. On the mouth, in front of the entire arena.

Lindsey grasped his jersey to hold on while people snapped pictures around them. She decided she didn't care, because Nelson didn't seem to either.

When he broke off, he said, "I need to do some interviews."

"Okay, we'll meet you outside."

He pressed his mouth against hers in a briefer kiss, then he released her, and soon he was swallowed up by the media.

Lindsey stared after him for a moment, but the crowd only grew more chaotic. So she turned to find Becca. They made their way out of the arena and into the parking lot.

"That was crazy," Becca said with a laugh.

Lindsey was happy to breathe in the fresh air away from the throngs of people. "Think we can find his truck?"

"Sure, it will be in the same place as always since he gets here so early."

Right. Lindsey knew that, but her head was still spinning.

They waited over an hour for Nelson to come out. Lindsey didn't mind. She and Becca sat on the bed of his truck and chatted about Becca's job, and Lindsey ended up telling her about the lawsuit against her former firm and some of the details about Paul Locker.

Becca was incredulous at the story, and Lindsey had to admit that it was nice to talk about it with another woman. Girlfriends had been mostly nonexistent for Lindsey, since she'd never had time, or made the time, to hang out with friends.

"There he is," Becca said. "Finally!" she called to Nelson. "What took you so long?"

Lindsey looked over to where he'd come out of the arena. The grin on his face said everything, and she couldn't be more excited for him.

"Just accepting a few accolades, nothing much," he teased.

Becca laughed, and he used his key fob to unlock the truck. Becca scrambled off the bed and headed for the passenger door.

Lindsey kept her gaze on Nelson. His freshly showered

look always woke up the butterflies in her stomach. He carried his duffle, and as he approached the truck bed, she stayed put.

"Thanks for waiting," he said, setting the duffle next to her, then zipping it open.

He smelled great, and if Becca weren't in the cab of the truck in full view, Lindsey might have given him another congratulatory kiss.

"Here," Nelson said, taking out a hockey jersey from the duffle. He shook it out. "I can wash it if you want, but it's yours."

Lindsey stared at the jersey. "That's your game jersey."

"Yeah."

She met his gaze. "You can't give that to me. It's probably worth a lot of money, or maybe your coach will want to put it in a display case or something."

Nelson didn't look away from her. "I want you to have it."

She took the jersey. It was slightly damp and smelled like the hockey arena. "I don't know what to say," she said in a quiet voice.

"You don't have to say anything." He stepped closer and rested his hands on her hips.

She set the jersey on her lap. "Nelson . . . I think you should keep it. You're going to regret giving it away. I mean, it represents history for you and for the Falcons."

"It wouldn't have happened if not for you," he said in a low voice. He moved closer now, stepping between her legs. She felt surrounded by his warmth as he rested his hands on her thighs.

"You can't say that either," she said. "You did all the work."

His lips quirked, and he slid his hands up to her waist, then tugged her against him. "A good percentage of sports is mental, and you helped me with that."

Lindsey wanted to demand clarification, but Nelson kissed her. The touch of his mouth against hers sent a warm shiver through her entire body. She wound her arms about his neck and let him take her into another realm.

The sound of a door opening reached them, and Becca said, "I'm still here. Waiting in the truck. And I'm hungry."

Nelson smiled against Lindsey's mouth. "Sorry about my sister. She can be demanding."

Lindsey moved her hands to his shoulders, then over his biceps and down his arms. "She's right. We should go." She peeled his hands from her waist.

Nelson sighed, then helped her down from the truck bed. He shut the back hatch, then they walked to the driver's side, where Lindsey climbed in first, followed by Nelson.

"Just wait until you see what we did to your place," Becca announced cheerfully.

He released a groan. "Don't tell me you used confetti."

Becca laughed. "You'll have to wait and see."

Nelson backed the truck out of its space, then reached for Lindsey's hand and held it all the way to his condo.

Twenty-four

Nelson looked around his condo. Boxes lined one wall, and the place looked even more bare than usual. Everything was packed—well, except for a few kitchen items like forks, plates, and cups. Those would be last. He'd be leaving Vegas in a couple of hours, and the only thing left to do was talk to Coach. Then Nelson would pick up the moving trailer on the way back to the condo. One of his neighbors had agreed to help him load furniture.

There was no use putting it off any longer; the moment had arrived.

He left the condo and headed for his truck. The drive to the arena sped by, and every light he hit was green. It was like some outside force was endorsing his decision. Nelson found Coach in his office, where he'd knew he'd be. He wore a button-down with his sleeves rolled up, and his receding hairline exposed a shiny scalp.

"What brings you in, Nelson?" Coach said, standing to shake his hand. "Everything okay with your knee?"

"Sure, it's fine," Nelson said. "Can I talk to you for a few minutes?"

"Of course." Coach indicated for Nelson to take a seat, while he moved to sit down again.

"First, I want to tell you how much I appreciate everything you've done for me," Nelson said. "You've been a great coach, and I've had opportunities with the Falcons that I wouldn't have gotten anywhere else."

Coach leaned forward. "You quitting on me, Nelson?"

Nelson swallowed. "My contract was fulfilled over a year ago, and I'm taking a break. Might end up with the Coyotes in a year or so, once John Sparks retires."

Coach stared at him. "You're kidding."

"Not kidding."

"The Coyotes were almost dead last in the league this year," Coach said, his voice growing edgy. "You just won the freakin' Stanley Cup, and you want to transfer to a deadbeat team?"

"They got Walton and Smith in a trade."

Coach shook his head. "What are they offering?"

"Three."

"You're making five million a year now, and you're willing to give up two million . . . for *what*? Because some of your teammates pissed you off during the playoffs?"

Nelson clenched his jaw. "There's more to life than hockey, Coach, and when you find it, you'll understand." He rose from the chair. "My lawyer will be in contact to wrap things up."

Coach slammed his fist on his desk. "Don't do this, Nelson. Take the whole damn summer off if you want to, but come back to Vegas."

"Thanks for the offer," he said. "But I've made up my mind."

Coach closed his eyes and exhaled. "Go on, get out of here."

So Nelson did. Not exactly how he wanted his last talk with Coach to turn out. Nelson supposed there might be a phone call later, but it didn't matter much now.

On the way across the parking lot, his phone rang. For a half second, he thought it might be Coach, but Dawson Harris's name flashed across the screen. Last time Dawson had called him, the news hadn't been good.

"Hello?" Nelson answered. "Is something wrong?"

"Nothing's wrong," Dawson said. "I was just calling to tell you that you'd better treat her right."

Nelson stopped by his truck. "Lindsey? What's going on?"

"She's on her way to Vegas," Dawson said. "Canceled her lease this morning and said she's flying out to tell you in person. She's going to relocate to live closer to you."

The breath left Nelson. "When did she leave?"

"A couple of hours ago," Dawson said. "So she should be landing soon. If she knew I was making this call, she'd kill me. But I felt like I needed to give you a heads-up so that you can be the man she thinks you are."

Nelson closed his eyes as his mind spun in a dozen different directions. "Do you know her flight information?"

"No," Dawson said. "Mind telling me what you're going to do when she tells you she's changing her life for you?"

Nelson took a deep breath and told Dawson about his resignation from the Falcons.

Dawson let out a low whistle. "Wow, really?" He chuckled. "I guess Lindsey will be getting the surprise of her life."

Nelson's stomach was in too many knots to find any humor in the situation.

"So does Lindsey's decision change yours?" Dawson asked after a moment.

"No," Nelson said immediately. "I'm done with the Falcons. Have been for a while, but meeting Lindsey gave me the push I needed to make the decision."

"Sounds like you've got some convincing to do on Lindsey's behalf," Dawson said.

"Wish me luck," Nelson said.

Dawson chuckled again. "I don't think you're gonna need it, man."

Nelson climbed into his truck after hanging up with Dawson. What were the chances? He'd been planning on showing up in Pine Valley and surprising Lindsey, but now she'd be at his place soon. His pulse thundered as he drove to the rental place and got a trailer hitched up to his truck.

There was no sign of Lindsey yet when he arrived at his condo, and he didn't know if he had a few minutes or an hour. So he did the only thing he could think of—paced the rooms until someone knocked on the door.

The sound made his pulse jump even though he was pretty sure it was her. He wasn't interested in pretending to be surprised or acting like he didn't know why she'd show up unexpectedly at his place. Besides, when he opened the door, he could practically see her nervousness. She didn't even step forward to hug him.

"Hi," she said, her voice breathless as she clasped her hands in front of her.

"Lindsey," he said. She was dressed in one of her business suits and strappy black heels, her hair pulled back from her face. Reminding him of when he'd first met her. There was that vulnerable look in her eyes again. "You're here."

"Surprise," she said, then bit her lip. "Um . . . can I come in?"

"Of course." He opened the door wider and stepped aside. She had no luggage with her, only a purse strapped over one shoulder.

Lindsey walked in, then stopped and looked around. "You're . . . *moving*?" She turned to face him, those clear blue eyes of hers cloudy with confusion.

"I am."

She looked away from him, then back. "Okay, I need to get this out fast, because I think I made a really big mistake. I should have thought this through more." She laughed, but it held no humor. "I didn't even bring a bag with me. And obviously you've made some significant plans that will probably make what I've come to tell you moot—"

"Lindsey," he cut in, stepping toward her.

She stepped back, her eyes filling with tears. "I'm sorry, I thought there was more between us, when there obviously isn't—"

Nelson moved forward again and grasped her hands. "Dawson called me about an hour ago. He told me you were coming."

She blinked several times, then exhaled as if she was trying to gain control of her emotions. "He did? So you know . . . everything?"

"I know enough," Nelson said, drawing her closer.

Her face flushed with embarrassment, and she closed her eyes. "Oh no."

"I want you to read something," he said, releasing one of her hands and pulling out his cell from his pocket. He pulled up his email app, then opened the SENT file. He clicked on one of the most recent emails he'd sent to Mr. Brown, the Coyotes' head coach. "Read this."

Lindsey's brows drew together, and she took the phone from him. It was a short email that outlined his acceptance of the offer to play for the Coyotes.

She must have read it multiple times, because it took her a few moments to reply. "You're transferring? Where are the Coyotes located?"

"About a two-hour drive from Pine Valley."

Her gaze snapped up to meet his. Her eyes filled with tears again. "What are you saying, Nelson? And be very, very clear."

He took the phone back, then raised his hand to touch her face. "Things have been rough with the Falcons for the past eighteen months. I didn't realize how messed up things were until I was injured and kept away from the team for a few weeks. Even though I didn't want to deal with an injury, it was a relief in a way. I started to think more seriously about transferring, especially since my five-year contract has been up for a while." He took a breath and slid his hand behind her neck. She wasn't pulling away, but she wasn't moving closer either. "But then I met you . . . And I fell in love with you, Lindsey."

Her lips parted in an exhale.

"I *am* in love with you," he said. "Being with you made me realize that I was missing a lot more than just respect from teammates and a coach who's willing to listen to my concerns. I was missing fulfillment, happiness, companionship." He touched her nose, and her lips curved. "I've been playing hockey since I was a kid, and it's been my life for as long as I remember. But I want more. I want to live closer to you. I don't have all the answers of how the nuts and bolts will work out, but I'm done with Vegas, babe. You can tell Dawson not to sell your office lease, because I need you back in Pine Valley with me. Or it's going to be one hell of a long summer."

Tears trailed down Lindsey's cheeks as she stared at him.

"I was going to show up in Pine Valley tonight to break the news," he said, "but you beat me to it."

Lindsey half laughed, half sobbed, then threw her arms about his neck. He pulled her close as she clung to him.

"I love you too, Tyler Nelson," she whispered.

He closed his eyes as he breathed in her scent, letting her

words wash over and through him. "I love you, babe, so much."

Neither of them moved for several moments. Then she sighed and drew back to wipe at her tears.

"I didn't mean to make you cry," he said, using his thumb to help her.

Lindsey smiled. "I think I'm dreaming."

Nelson kissed her forehead. "It's no dream."

She took a steadying breath. "Are you sure about moving to Pine Valley? I mean, it's a huge change."

"It's the *right* change," Nelson said. "My career isn't all about me anymore, it's about us, sweetheart. Everything I do from now on is all for you."

Lindsey's mouth curved into a beautiful smile. "You're going to make me cry again."

He chuckled, then he cradled her face. He searched her blue eyes, finding only love and the sweetness that was Lindsey in her gaze. "Wanna road trip with me?" he asked.

Her expression turned coy. "Is that your moving trailer out there?"

"It is."

"Well, since I'm already here," she said, "I might as well come along for the ride."

He laughed. "Perfect." He leaned down, then he kissed her, long and slow. She twined her arms about his neck, kissing him back. Now that they'd be living in the same town, Nelson was looking forward to a lot more time with Lindsey, and a lot more kissing. So he might as well start it off right.

More Pine Valley Novels!

Heather B. Moore is a four-time *USA Today* bestselling author. She writes historical thrillers under the pen name H.B. Moore; her latest thrillers include *The Killing Curse* and *Breaking Jess*. Under the name Heather B. Moore, she writes romance and women's fiction. Her newest releases include the historical romances *Love is Come* and *Ruth*. She's also one of the coauthors of the *USA Today* bestselling series: A Timeless Romance Anthology. Heather writes speculative fiction under the pen name Jane Redd; releases include the Solstice series and *Mistress Grim*. Heather is represented by Dystel, Goderich & Bourret.

For book updates, sign up for Heather's email list: hbmoore.com/contact
Website: HBMoore.com
Facebook: Fans of H. B. Moore
Blog: MyWritersLair.blogspot.com
Instagram: @authorhbmoore
Twitter: @HeatherBMoore